I0568094

It's no ordinary morning when Toni Starr arrives at Zach's garage. Flat broke, with a past she won't share, Toni's instantly taken by such a potently virile man. Direct and unashamed, she tells him she's a motorcycle performance artist who needs work and knows motors.

Zach knows women, and Toni's unlike any he's met. Lushly sensuous, exceedingly assured, she'd easily be his match in business and bed. A provocative challenge that stirs him as nothing has since losing his wife. A chance he's reluctant to take, offering no more than a month's employment, then she'll have to be on her way.

The hours tick by. Each word and glance intensifies their denied yet escalating desire, forcing them to surrender to passion. Driven by carnal hunger, conquered by yearning, they face the unforeseen truth of Toni's past and a future neither of them expected.

The unauthorized reproduction or distribution of this copy-righted work is illegal. Criminal copyright infringement, including infringement without monetary gain, is investigated by the FBI and is punishable by up to 5 years in federal prison and a fine of $250,000.

This book is a work of fiction. Names, characters, places, and incidents either are products of the author's imagination or are used fictiously. Any resemblance to actual events or lo-cales or persons, living or dead, is entirely coincidental.

Sensual Stranger
Copyright © 2019 Tina Donahue
ISBN: 978-1-4874-2585-2
Cover art by Martine Jardin

All rights reserved. Except for use in any review, the repro-duction or utilization of this work in whole or in part in any form by any electronic, mechanical or other means, now known or hereafter invented, is forbidden without the written permission of the publisher.

Published by eXtasy Books Inc or
Devine Destinies, an imprint of eXtasy Books Inc

Look for us online at:
www.eXtasybooks.com or www.devinedestinies.com

Sensual Stranger

By

Tina Donahue

DEDICATION

To lovers everywhere who've found a second chance at happiness.

CHAPTER ONE

Toni Starr propped her shoulder against a storefront on the deserted street, ignoring her thirst, the heat, and her weariness. For too many years, she'd yearned for a place to call her own where she'd always belong.

Wouldn't happen in this small town.

Hopefully, the automotive service shop across the street would open before a merchant, or worse, a cop showed up and ran her off.

Please, not that. She couldn't walk another step.

The metal doors for Brody's Auto Repair rattled upward for the day's business.

Her pulse picked up.

A man inside the building gripped a clipboard holding numerous papers. The bays were empty except for cars, no other employees having arrived. Nor were there any customers waiting at the glass door in front.

An old Tim McGraw tune poured from inside, the singer's resonant voice subdued by heartache.

Her fatigue and uncertainty retreated, replaced by interest in the man. Surely over six feet, he looked early thirties or so and filled out his white cotton tee and worn jeans nicely.

She managed a small breath.

Solid didn't begin to address his broad shoulders, sculpted chest, and muscular biceps. Faded denim hugged his powerful legs, and the meaty bulge behind his fly.

Her mouth watered despite the worsening heat and the mess she was in.

He turned to the side, taking his best parts from her view.

Disappointed, she craned her neck.

Blond locks streaked his light brown hair, worn longish on the top and sides, wonderfully tousled as if he'd finger-combed it after he'd rolled out of bed.

He certainly hadn't shaved.

Short, dark bristles shadowed his cheeks, firm jaw, and upper lip, his beginning beard virile and wholly masculine, complementing his rich, sensuous mouth.

Her stomach fluttered, and her thoughts roamed at being in his strong arms, safe from hurt the world seemed determined to inflict. His big body pressed close, hard, and protective.

He strode to a Saturn in the middle bay, favoring his right leg. Not a limp exactly, more a hesitation in his fluid gait. The way a man would walk after straining the muscles in his calf.

Pain flickered across his handsome features, followed by what might have been sorrow or regret.

As quickly as the emotion surfaced, it passed. His face grew impassive, all business, his attention torn between the car and his clipboard, then something to the left in the work area. Crossing it, he again depended more on his right leg, stopped at a small refrigerator, and pulled out a bottled water. He placed it on a waist-high metal cabinet that likely held tools. Forearms on it, he bent his head to the papers, reading the first then the next.

She couldn't tell if he owned the place or simply managed it. More importantly, whether he'd listen to her and have the authority to do what she needed.

Desperation returned. Perspiration trickled down her cheek. She squinted at the unforgiving sun streaming over distant mountains and past the flat-faced buildings on her side. Those rays hit the garage full-on, bathing it in the light, seeming to direct her.

Go on. Before anyone else shows up.

Queasy with uncertainty, she pushed away from the gift shop. The small downtown area was quiet, the other storefront businesses closed. No cars rolled down the narrow two-lane street. No locals or visitors noticed her. Nor did he. His focus remained on the papers, shoulders relaxed.

He pushed a wayward lock behind his ear.

She liked his hair and battered cowboy boots. They fit him as well as everything else did in this town. He belonged. She didn't.

Too late to turn back now.

With the sun at her back and her heart pounding, she trudged toward him.

Zach Brody yawned and reached for his bottled water.

A gentle breeze wafted in, bearing an unexpected fragrance: a decadent mixture of leather and a flowery scent. Bold yet gentle. Hard yet soft.

A shadow fell across the metal cabinet and today's work orders.

Forgetting his water, he turned.

The outside light silhouetted a woman, the rays skimming her hair, cut in a layered style, the color so black there were faint blue highlights. The glare from behind hid her features but not her full length.

Tallish, at five-nine or so, she had nice curves and long legs.

Heat rushed from his chest to his groin, and his cock stirred, proving what he already knew. Although his heart had been immune to love for nearly two years, and the complications it represented, especially loss, the rest of him still lusted.

His chest tightened, and his mouth went dry.

She lowered something to the concrete floor. "Are you the

owner?"

New warmth arrowed down to his shaft, making it even stiffer and tightening his balls. To say her voice was smoky was an understatement. The deep, throaty pitch reminded him how a woman sounds once she's sated by sex—a long, hard, satisfying fuck on a blistering summer afternoon.

She stepped to the left.

The sun hit him full in the eyes. He squinted and pushed away from the cabinet, pausing at the pain and stiffness in his left leg. Gritting his teeth, he gave his limb a moment to relax before he regarded her.

His heartbeat quickened.

She wore snug leather pants and a jacket, both garments supple and black, the outfit covering her from toes to throat. He couldn't hide his surprise. Although it wasn't yet eight o'clock, late spring mornings in this part of Arizona heated up fast. From a cool sixty degrees at sunrise, the temperature had already reached the mid-seventies. Hadn't she noticed?

Her biker boots were definitely kickass. A helmet dangled from her left hand. She'd lowered a fringed saddlebag to the floor.

Her leather jacket molded itself to her full, ripe breasts.

They rose slightly each time she inhaled.

He remembered to breathe and lifted his gaze to hers.

Something inside him shifted, heightening his senses, his awareness of colors and textures pronounced.

Her pale skin had a dewy quality only youth could provide, telling him she couldn't be more than mid-twenties. Her blue-green eyes were amazing. There simply wasn't another word to fit such an unusual shade. Coupled with her raven hair and the black leather, he couldn't stop staring. She wasn't the most beautiful woman he'd ever seen or even conventionally pretty.

Rather, she was decidedly interesting and effortlessly

sensual without seeming to realize it, while her gaze . . . Although direct, it was oddly vulnerable, encouraging a man to do whatever she proposed.

Perspiration slid from her temple to her downy cheek. Damp hair stuck to it. She glanced at the water he'd left on the cabinet.

He twisted off the cap and offered her the beverage along with an answer to what she'd asked. A question he just recalled. "Yeah, I'm the owner. Zach Brody."

Her gaze flicked from the bottle to him and back. "Thanks." She took the water

Their fingers touched.

Nerve endings fired, stealing his breath and stalling his next comment. He released the bottle and glanced past for her bike.

Wasn't out front.

Maybe it broke down farther up the street. That had to be why she was here.

Eyes closed, head tilted back, she enjoyed long gulps of the chilled water, her slender throat bobbing with each swallow.

A faint blue vein ran down her neck. He had an insane urge to touch it.

She stopped drinking, the almost empty bottle still to her mouth. A delighted whimper escaped her.

Zach figured he should get her another water, in case she wanted more, but couldn't move.

A wayward breeze ruffled her hair. The town stirred. Tires from a car or pickup hummed down the street. A vehicle door thudded. Faint voices drifted from up the street, around Hector and Em's diner.

The radio in here played a LeAnn Rimes tune. Her clear, powerful voice swept across the work area as she sang about living without her man.

The young woman upended the bottle and finished the last

drop. Eyes still closed, she brought the container down and pressed it to her forehead, her cheek, her throat, moaning softly at its cool, damp bite.

Warmth roared through him, along with too much need he didn't want to feel or address. Shaking off his arousal, he backed up to the fridge and pulled out another water.

She ran her tongue over her plump bottom lip.

Warning himself not to stare, he stopped well short of her and put out his hand for the empty bottle.

She offered it with a smile.

He returned it easily, something rushing between them, inviting him closer.

Surprised at his reaction, he locked his knees to keep from moving and killed his grin. Since losing Meg, he hadn't—or rather his mind hadn't—responded this strongly to any woman and certainly not a customer.

He took the empty bottle from her and offered the new one, behaving as the professional he was supposed to be rather than a hormone-soaked teen.

Something flickered in her eyes.

If he had to guess, he would have said disappointment or resignation, certainly embarrassment. Her cheeks had colored.

She took the bottle. "Thanks. You're sure you don't mind if I have this?"

Her hesitation touched him. Fuck, it was only water. "Not at all. If you want another after that one, just say the word. What's wrong with your bike?"

After finishing her swallow, she held the bottle to her cheek and inhaled deeply. Her lids slipped down. "My bike?"

"Your cycle."

She pressed the bottle to her neck. Water or perspiration slid beneath the leather, travelling to her breasts.

He cleared his throat but still had difficulty speaking.

"Whatever you drove to get here."

She lifted the bottle to her temple and shook her head gently.

He didn't understand. "You did drive here, right?"

"No." She finished another long sip and swiped her hand across her mouth. Water clung tenaciously to the corners.

He had trouble concentrating. "So how'd you get here?"

"I hitched a ride." She rested the bottle on her left wrist. Her black helmet swung back and forth like a pendulum. "And then I walked."

Dark brown dust coated her biker boots and the bottom of her leather pants. "From where?"

"The next town over. I don't recall its name."

The only town in the vicinity happened to be several miles north and not connected to this one by a local road. The sole way to get to it by car was over the interstate. On foot, as the crow flies, one had to hike through a wash bordered by chaparral thick with cottonwood trees, junipers, snakes, scorpions, and lizards. Which she'd apparently done.

He hadn't a clue why. The other town had a repair shop. His was better, but only locals would know that.

She definitely wasn't from around here.

A drop slid down her chin, hung on for a moment then fell to her jacket near her right breast.

With concentrated effort, he focused on their conversation and forced himself to sound far more casual than he felt. "And you're here in my garage because?"

"I'm flat broke. I have nowhere else to go. I need a job."

CHAPTER TWO

At Toni's confession, surprise registered in his eyes, their color more amber than hazel, making his long lashes and eyebrows seem even darker, erotic, dangerous.

The way he'd looked at her as their gazes first met.

Carnal promise filled his face then, the slight acceleration in his breathing, his increasing intensity, proving his arousal.

He'd checked his response. Not because he was married — he wore no ring. His too-early arrival at the shop further convinced her he was currently unattached or divorced.

Maybe he'd tamed his reaction so as not to spook her. She liked that, admiring restraint in a man, being able to control himself around a female, respecting boundaries until she invited him inside, understanding the difference between right and wrong.

Joe hadn't appreciated the distinction, nor had he cared. Propriety, common decency, her saying 'no' had meant nothing to him. And so she'd had to leave. There'd been no other choice.

Sorrow and fury rose within her, which she pushed back quickly, not allowing it to wound. Too many years had passed, too many miles. Sometimes she found it hard to remember the many places she'd stopped in or to consider where she might be a month from now and at some distant time in the future.

Until then, she was here with Zach.

For the time being.

Not wanting to think about being turned down, she

indulged in this pleasant moment instead. His clean, soapy scent tightened her nipples and weakened every other part of her. To bury her face in his neck, savor his heat and fragrance, have him hold her, talk to her, get to know and like her would be so sweet.

She wasn't asking for the moon or forever after. Early on, she'd learned that fantasy didn't exist. A little kindness and friendship wouldn't be so hard to give, would it?

He glanced at the street.

If he was looking for her bike, he'd never find it there, which would lead him to ask where it was. She'd tell him in time when she had no other choice.

"A job?" Giving her no chance to respond, he shook his head. "Sorry, but I don't need a receptionist. I handle the customers."

"Who works on the vehicles?"

He lifted his dark eyebrows. "My two mechanics."

"That aren't here. I am."

His eyebrows kept inching up as his gaze drifted down her body, settling on her breasts. "You're a mechanic?"

"I can repair cars or cycles." Her next words spilled out before she could stop them. "Lucky taught me."

"Lucky?"

"Just give me a chance to prove myself." She rested her helmet on the cabinet. The metal vibrated slightly from its weight. "I'm the best damn mechanic there is."

Before he could challenge her statement, she backed toward the red Saturn SC2, a two-door she guessed to be eighteen years old. Paint bubbled on its roof. Part of the rubber molding on the passenger door was missing. "What's wrong with it?"

He leaned against the cabinet, feet crossed at the ankles, arms folded over his broad chest.

Stalling for an answer?

Without warning, a slow, sexy grin spread across his face.

9

"You mean the best damn mechanic there is doesn't know?"

She liked his teasing. She could spend days with his smile, content to be the reason for it.

Pretending offense, she lifted her chin. "Even though I can fix anything you put in front of me, unfortunately, I'm not psychic."

His smile faded, his caution returning.

She pointed to his clipboard. "Can I see the work order?"

The papers fluttered in the mild breeze. He didn't offer them to her. A song reached its last chords on the radio. The station's peppy deejay counted down the artists whose recordings he'd just played. Finished, he extolled the hearty breakfasts offered at the Last Chance Diner.

Zach was going to tell her to get lost. She could feel it and had to stop him. "Look, I need the job, and you obviously could use the help." She gestured to the filled bays and toward the fenced lot she'd seen earlier while awaiting his arrival. Vehicles filled it, too.

He didn't glance that way or respond.

Worry gnawed at her, giving her the courage she needed to see this through and win unless he physically escorted her out or called the cops.

He didn't seem that kind of man. Beneath his surprise at learning she was broke, empathy and kindness had shone in his eyes. She inclined her head to the Saturn. "What's wrong with it?"

He grabbed the clipboard, flipped through several pages, and read. "Doesn't run good."

She laughed. It sounded a bit shrill. "That's your mechanic's assessment?"

Fighting a smile, he shook his head. "That's what Amy Dobson said. Tucson address. Must be a tourist." He ran his finger down the sheet. "The engine's hard to start, and it runs rough."

"It's older than a two thousand two, right?"

His eyes widened. "Two thousand to be exact."

With a shrug, she made an educated guess. "Needs plugs."

Zach's eyebrows didn't lower.

Maybe she should clarify. "Spark plugs."

"Yeah, I know what they are." He tossed the clipboard on the cabinet. The metal vibrated loudly. "Lucky teach you about spark plugs?"

She cursed her big mouth. "Care to make a bet that I'm right?"

He ran his thumb over his bristly jaw. "Thought you didn't have any money."

"I don't. I'm willing to bet my job here if I'm wrong, which I'm not."

He didn't comment.

She smiled. "Scared you're mistaken about me?"

Color rose to his face, darkening his bronzed complexion. A car raced down the otherwise placid street. He looked over at the noise. "It's not a matter of that."

"Then, let me show you what I can do." Not waiting for his response or rejection, she unzipped her leather jacket and pulled it off.

He stared at her black tank top. The tight, stretchy material clung to her and stopped short of her waist, revealing a sliver of skin above her pants.

She joined him, folded her jacket inside out and draped it over her helmet, close to his side. "Where do you keep your ratchet wrenches and rags?"

Renewed amazement played across his face.

"I just want to take a look." She lifted her hands in concession. "I won't hurt it."

He grew thoughtful then pushed away from the cabinet and pulled open a drawer.

As she grabbed the tool, he tossed a rust-colored rag on the cabinet.

"Thanks." She smiled. "Excuse me." She leaned past him to take the rag.

Their biceps touched.

He inhaled deeply.

A delicious shiver ran through her. She lifted her face to his. Dark brown ringed his irises, enhancing the gold. Green flecks added more color. He wore the look he had upon first seeing her. Purely male. Nearly predatory. Her heart thrummed in appreciation.

Interest flared in his eyes but died quickly. He stepped back, breaking their contact.

She hid her regret. "Is it always so hot around here?"

He rubbed his neck. "Only after the sun rises."

"Tell me about it." She kept her mood breezy. "At dawn, I was freezing. Now though . . ." Giving him no chance to comment, she returned to the Saturn and addressed it. "Okay, cupcake, let's have a look under your skirts. Don't worry, mama won't hurt you."

She opened the hood.

What in the fuck are you doing? Tell her to leave.

Words wouldn't come to Zach. Her slender, toned arms were as pale and dewy as the rest of her. When she'd taken off her leather jacket, her fragrance drifted over him, making him damn near dizzy. Who in the hell was she? What was she doing here? In Indulgence of all places?

He stepped closer. Pain shot down his leg. For once, the agony wasn't so bad. Gaping at her comforted his battered muscles better than Advil.

She bent to the motor and carefully wiped the area around the plugs.

Like she knew what she was doing. *Who are you?* For some reason, he wanted to know everything about her when he'd never been this curious about a stranger. "What's your name?"

She continued working, not bothering to glance over. "Look at my jacket and you'll see . . . if you want."

He did, liking how she teased, but he was still confused.

The moment he lifted her garment from the cabinet, her flowery scent mixed with leather washed over him. His throat tightened, making it impossible to swallow, and his cock pressed against his fly, wanting out.

Doing his best to ignore his lust, he searched for and found the inside label.

She laughed. A deep, throaty sound that plumped his balls. "Not there. Look on the outside, the back."

He preferred watching her.

Their gazes locked.

The air grew heavier than it had been. Sounds faded. Colors brightened.

Say something.

He didn't know what.

She looked like she might speak, but didn't, and broke contact first. Head tilted to the engine, she used the ratchet with skill, as though it had always been a part of her hand. She didn't appear to mind the grease, oil, and muck found in any garage.

She turned her face to the side but didn't look at him. "Do you see it?"

Zach had no idea what she was talking about, and then he remembered . . . her name. Black rhinestones decorated the jacket back. He grinned. The gems caught the light, winked it back, and spelled out letters in a modified script.

He read out loud, "Toni Starr." The name sounded comfortable on his lips, though not entirely real.

"That's me."

No woman he knew wore neck-to-toe leather along with a possibly fake name printed in sparkly letters on her jacket.

She had to be a performer. A stripper?

Are you nuts? A stripper who knows auto repair? "What's your line of work?"

"Auto mechanic, once you hire me."

He didn't try to stop his smile. "What was your line of work yesterday?"

"I was looking for a job. I went through two towns north of here."

Those garage names flashed in his mind. He lowered her jacket to the cabinet and pinched his nose, imagining her walking the five or so miles between those two places unless she hitched a ride. "What was your job last week?"

Laughter spilled from her.

He suspected she enjoyed dodging his questions. "Come on. Give."

"If you insist. I'm a motorcycle performance artist."

Zach dropped his hand and forgot what he'd intended to say.

Bent at the waist over the motor, she looked at him, while her sweet ass . . .

Perspiration ran down his chest and back. She'd assumed the perfect position for him to mount her, just like in a horny male fantasy or a triple X-rated film about a garage owner and a motorcycle performance artist.

His balls hurt, and the skin on his cock seemed ready to split with nowhere for his erection to go, no place to find relief except in his mind. There, all hell broke loose, images rising to show him unbuttoning and unzipping her leather pants, peeling them from her plush hips and succulent ass.

The leather would surely resist, clinging to her flesh, not wanting to leave its fragrant home. She'd wiggle slightly, helping him. The movement would deliver more of her sweet, sultry scent.

With her pants to her knees, he'd stroke the furrow

between her cheeks and dip beneath her thong. It had to be black to match her other clothing unless it was red. *Oh, yeah.* Red silk bordered with black lace.

New pictures unwound in his brain, creating scenes showing irresistible lust. Him caressing her hot, moist flesh. Her damp pussy slick with arousal. Her vaginal lips plump with need. The decadent aroma of her female musk beneath her flowery scent and the leather. Him mounting her, burrowing his cock into her narrow, heated sheath, tunneling as deep as he could go. Burying himself. Losing himself.

In a woman who wasn't anything like Meg.

Memories of his late wife drifted close: her long blonde hair, brown eyes, the dimples in each cheek when she smiled or laughed. He tensed against the familiar pain that always accompanied his thoughts about her. This morning, grief was on the mild side. Time had blunted the emptiness and the blame he'd heaped upon himself.

Not certain whether to feel relieved or guiltier than before, he stared at Toni. A stranger who wore her name—fake or otherwise—on her jacket, was flat broke and had worked as a motorcycle performance artist. The job title nearly made him grin. "You're a what?"

"Daredevil." She spoke casually as most would as they explained being teachers, waitresses, or convenience store clerks, not daredevils. "Next month, when the circuit starts up again, I'll be following it as I always do."

Until then, she needed a job here, walking through the heat, brush, and God knew what else to reach his business. "What happened to your bike? Did someone steal it?"

Her face clouded, her playful mood gone. She focused on the motor rather than him. "In a manner of speaking."

Zach wondered where she'd learned to dodge questions so well. "If someone took it, shouldn't you be talking to the sheriff or the local police and your insurance agent?"

"Nope."

"Why not?"

She gripped the wrench so tightly, her knuckles blanched.

He should have backed off, but couldn't. "What happened? Did someone you know take it?"

"I wish." She sagged. "Before you ask anything else, I can't call any insurance agent since I don't have one. I can't afford to buy the product. And the sheriff's the one who has my bike." Straightened, she gestured to the car's guts. "It does need new plugs. There's a nasty oil leak in there that's going to cause them to fail eventually. They're coated with the stuff."

Zach couldn't have cared less about the motor. "Why does the sheriff have your bike?"

"The usual reasons."

His frustration fought with his amusement. She was really something. What exactly, he wasn't altogether certain. However, he couldn't deny how much he enjoyed her verbal gymnastics. "Which are?"

She wiped her fingers on the rag. "I was at that farm supply store north of here, putting on a performance in the lot." She snuck a look at him then examined her nails and scrubbed them with the cloth. "I wasn't hurting anything. I wasn't anywhere near the damned store. I was just trying to make some cash until I can get back on the circuit."

She shrugged. "The crowd was building up really well, and then a deputy appeared out of nowhere. He wanted proof of insurance, which I didn't have, and my permit to perform, which I also didn't have." She rolled her eyes. "Before I knew it, he was calling a towing company and impounding my bike. When I couldn't pay the fine, the judge sentenced me to three days in jail and told me they'd keep my bike and driver's license until I could pay the fees and get insurance."

Her nonchalance about the matter surprised him, along

with something else. "You couldn't call your folks to have them bail you out?"

Her features darkened. She averted her gaze and watched the few cars going down the street. "Every day my bike's in impound, they tack on more storage fees. What a racket, huh? I figure after a month here, fixing these babies," she rapped her knuckles against the Saturn, "I'll have enough to get my bike, some cheapo insurance, and take off, just in time for the start of the season."

Sounded reasonable for someone who led such an unconventional life and apparently did it alone.

Why that disturbed him, he hadn't a clue. She was a stranger. As interesting as the last few minutes had been, it wasn't his job to help her.

He was curious about her family, though, if she was on the outs with her parents. And who the fuck was Lucky? Zach guessed an ex, either boyfriend or husband.

She lowered the hood. "You need the help."

The cars in the bay evidenced as much, along with those in the lot. Work that kept him busy at night after his mechanics left, sparing him from thinking too much, wondering what might have been if he hadn't lost Meg.

"Sorry." He cleared the catch in his voice, emotion he forced down. "I can't hire you."

Sadness pinched her features. "Sure you can." She spoke softly, without accusation. "But you won't."

He wanted to explain, to look away, but couldn't.

Their silence grew, allowing other sounds to intrude. Carrie Underwood's latest hit played on the radio. A jet rumbled overhead on its journey west, possibly to Los Angeles or Hawaii. Children's voices, shrill with excitement, urged their parents to hurry down the street.

"It's okay." Toni gave him a resigned smile. "At least I gave it a shot." She cleaned the wrench. After putting the tool back in its drawer, she folded the rag and left it on top of the cabinet.

Each movement delivered her scent. Perspiration beaded on her throat. A small mole graced her left biceps, a solitary mark amidst all that pale skin.

His heart beat too quickly. Unable to stop himself, he wanted to know about her. "Where will you go now?"

She lifted her narrow shoulders. "The next repair shop that might need help. Do you mind?" She gestured to a container with hand cleaning wipes.

Zach shook his head.

She scrubbed her hands, pitched the wipe in the trash, and reached for her jacket.

He touched her wrist, stopping her. Her skin was silkier than he'd imagined. Pleasure jolted through him. He struggled to calm himself. "You said you were flat broke. Does that mean you have no money at all?"

Her mouth trembled, showing him the fear she tried so hard to hide. His gut ached at how lost she looked.

She pushed away the emotion and grew aloof. "If I did have funds, I wouldn't be here."

Not good enough. He wanted a real explanation. What in the fuck could have happened in her life to have brought her to this sorry point? "When was the last time you ate?"

Bewilderment crossed her face. "At the shelter last night."

"You're staying there?"

"Not again. It's hardly permanent housing. There are a lot of mothers with little kids who need the facilities more than I do."

Zach placed her jacket on an adjacent counter.

Her face lit up. "You're hiring me after all?"

He cupped her elbow and stroked her smooth, hot skin, the movement independent of his brain and good sense. "I'm buying you breakfast." It was the least he could do. "Come on."

CHAPTER THREE

Zach's sensuous touch, firm caress, and restrained strength undid Toni. She couldn't recall the last time a man had treated her with such respect and consideration. Desire built, making her warmer than she already was, pushing away aching loneliness, encouraging her to edge closer to him.

She stopped herself before she did. She needed a job, not him to touch her, no matter how pleasant. She required work, not simply breakfast, despite how hungry she was. Had he heard her growling belly? *Probably.*

Lightly, he tightened his hold on her elbow. "Come on."

His gentle directive and obvious concern for her defeated Toni's refusal to accept his charity. She'd been tired and hungry in the past, though nothing like now. Sitting down and eating would be heaven. Having someone take care of her, making her feel wanted and safe, if only for a little while, was more than she could resist.

He directed her toward the street.

"Wait." She held back. "My saddlebag."

He glanced at it.

"It's all I have, along with my helmet and jacket." She hated to admit as much, but couldn't think of anything but the truth.

Dismay, rather than surprise, filled his face.

A young man strode into the garage. Probably early twenties, the guy had faded blue eyes and brown hair cut in a longish crew. The ends stuck straight up thanks to industrial-strength gel. A dagger-shaped silver earring decorated his left lobe, a small ring curled over his right nostril. Baggy jeans and a navy tee hung on his lean, youthful frame.

He scratched his cheek. "Mornin'."

Zach nodded.

The guy slid his gaze to her—or rather all over her—then to Zach cupping her elbow. His attention perked up at the scene.

Zach gave him a frosty look. "Put the lady's jacket, helmet, and saddlebag in my office."

"No." She touched Zach's arm. "I'm taking the bag."

The young man took them both in then settled on her breasts and remained there.

"Fine." Zach squeezed her elbow then spoke to the guy. "Robbie? Her helmet and jacket? My office?"

"Uh, sure." He gave her a quick, questioning smile. With her stuff in hand, he sauntered to the office but kept glancing back.

She kept her voice lowered. "Is he one of your mechanics?"

Zach nodded.

She wanted to ask if Robbie was good at his job, but didn't. It wouldn't change Zach's mind about her working here. Besides, she didn't want to push someone else out to give herself a chance, no matter her desperation.

Zach grabbed the carrying handles on her saddlebag and hauled it up.

"I'll take it." She wiggled her fingers.

Easily, he held it from her reach and studied its bulging contours. "It's much heavier than I thought it would be. What do you have in here?"

Her life. "Stuff that belongs to me."

He regarded her, seeming to expect more of an answer.

Toni liked him already for his teasing and offering to buy her breakfast, but she wasn't about to give an inch when it came to her present or past. "I can carry it."

"Not while I'm here." He guided her toward the street,

totally in charge, though not in a bad way.

Her belly fluttered. His kindness mixed with dominance was the best of both worlds when it came to a man. Someone who knew what he wanted but wouldn't insist . . . he'd be fair and kind. She wondered if this was how he was in bed with a woman he wanted. Demanding, yet giving. Dangerous yet safe. Playing wicked carnal games, then caressing her gently afterwards, his tender kisses delivering her to sleep, because he was a good guy.

Heat flooded her face that had nothing to do with the sun bearing down. She tried to focus on anything other than Zach, but kept circling back to kneeling before him, obedient to his desires and hers, unbuttoning his jeans, lowering the zipper.

She could almost hear the metal rasp.

Delight pulsed through her.

"Toni?"

Her fantasy stalled. She marveled at his beautiful eyes and masculine features, wondering what it would be like to stroke his bristly cheeks and tunnel her hands through his silky hair. Several locks dangled over his forehead. The breeze played with them. Lucky breeze. "What?"

He got a faraway look in his eyes then returned to the moment and glanced past her. "What do you like to eat? There's a diner to the right with the usual breakfast fare or a pancake house to the left."

With each choice he'd offered, his hold on her elbow tightened ever so slightly.

Far too conscious of his touch and everything else about him, she tried to distract herself. Wooden buildings crowded the street, each painted in bright primary colors. Firecracker reds, vivid blues, and buttercup yellows made the area cheery and welcoming. Most of the architecture sported an Old West look with flat fronts and fancy gold lettering on the windows.

The wind fluttered past, delivering bacon and cinnamon

scents. Her lids slid down at the heavenly aromas. At this point, she was hungry enough to eat grass. "Do you smell that? Where's it coming from?"

"The diner."

"Oh, there. Please."

"Good choice." His voice rumbled with pleasure.

She loved his honest and unguarded smile, but didn't want to stare too obviously and glanced past to the hard blue sky. There wasn't a cloud in sight to mar its perfection, only numerous blackbirds winging their way toward the mountains.

Hand on her arm, he led her up the street to what she guessed was the diner, his stride slow and uneven.

She glanced at his leg.

He looked straight ahead. "How long have you been here?"

"I don't know. Where's here?"

He chuckled.

Her heart made a funny leap at having made him laugh and the sexy crinkles at the corners of his eyes.

He slanted her a look. "You're in Arizona."

"Yeah, I know that. I meant, where's here?" With her free hand, she pointed down. "This town, city, whatever. I didn't see any signs coming in." She'd been too busy searching for a garage and stopped when she found his. "What's it called?"

"Indulgence."

"Get out."

Grinning, he inclined his head toward the other side of the street and the storefront windows she hadn't noticed earlier, having been too focused on her thirst, hunger, and fatigue. There was Indulgence Gifts, Indulgence Ice Cream Parlor, Indulgence Western Wear. "There has to be a story behind that name."

"Actually, a marketing plan. A few years back the city council consulted an advertising firm about ways to bring in more tourist dollars. The firm concluded a good start would be changing the name from Keanyville. They said Indulgence sounded like a town in an old Clint Eastwood movie and people would flock here."

Given the few cars on the street, it wasn't exactly rush hour in New York, but the parking spaces were filling up and what seemed to be tourists glanced in the shop windows. "Sounds like a plan. So nothing wild goes on here?"

He released her elbow and stopped at a street corner. A dark blue sedan passed the stop sign slower than a sloth. The elderly driver's face was mapped with wrinkles that deepened as she glared at Toni. Next, she frowned at Zach.

Offering an easy smile, he dipped his head in greeting.

The woman kept glancing over her shoulder at them as her vehicle rolled across the street.

Zach gestured Toni to the other side. "Define wild."

His question surprised her and brought to mind the men she'd known, each out for a good time—gambling, boozing, fucking—all indifferent about the future. As far as she was concerned, that made them more stupid than anything, afraid to grow up.

Wild was a man risking his heart, falling so hard he'd have no chance to recover and would hold her close every night, loving her to distraction . . . standing at her side, giving her a family and home.

Pitiless yearning rose. She shoved it back down. Indulgence was Zach's home. It would never be hers. No place would for long. "You tell me."

He slowed and stopped. Cars edged down the street, the passengers taking in the scenery. Bells tinkled on doors. Voices lifted in greeting.

She looked at him.

He held her gaze. "Whatever you want."

Her pulse leaped. For one crazy moment, she wondered if

he'd read her thoughts. "What do you mean?"

"I said I'm buying."

They'd reached the Last Chance Diner the deejay had talked about.

She pushed her foolish musing aside. "So you did." She cocked her head, a hard negotiator again. "Tell you what, hire me and I'll buy *you* breakfast."

He cuffed her wrist, folded her arm behind her back, and pulled her into him.

Her breath caught.

His strength, size, and bulk felt ungodly good, but she hadn't a clue what he was doing or why he chose this public spot to do it.

He stepped back, taking her with him.

Several middle-aged tourists barreled past, interrupting each other as they discussed today's plans, not watching where they were going.

Even with Zach keeping her out of their way, one man elbowed her arm.

She barely noticed the jab. She softened at Zach's clean scent, his powerful body against hers. His Adam's apple bounced from his hard swallow. Short, dark hairs graced his throat.

He pulled in a shallow breath. "We better go inside."

Liking how rough his voice sounded, she didn't move.

Neither did he.

What in the fuck are you doing?

Zach had no idea and didn't have enough willpower to resist the moment.

Toni's eyes and guileless expression held him captive. He felt he could reach whatever was in her soul when what he wanted to do was crawl all over her.

There it was—the unvarnished truth. He ached to screw

with her like he hadn't needed to fuck with a woman in nearly two years. That should have bothered or shamed him somehow and brought on guilt because of Meg.

At this moment, it did not. Animal instinct and raw male need erased everything else. Not only because of Toni's powerful sensuality but because he sensed how alone she was . . . as much as him.

Yesterday his solitude had hurt, though time had taken away some pain. Today, the isolation seemed unbearable, urging him to move on, to live, to take whatever he could — whatever she offered.

He couldn't. Not here. Certainly not with a woman who was a stranger and would soon be on her way.

With great effort, he released her and stepped back to open the diner door. Its bell tinkled. Aromas from strong coffee, sugar-cured bacon, and rich baked goods poured out, along with an old Kenny Rogers' tune and customers' voices.

At the sounds or the scents, Toni glanced up.

Fevered and restless, he wanted to kiss her, or run like crazy, or do some-fucking-thing, but couldn't budge. Her milky skin contrasted beautifully against her black tank top. The garment hugged her better than skin, causing her tightened nipples to poke against the stretchy fabric. Blood rushed to his groin and pooled in his cock.

Her stomach growled, loud and long.

She pressed her hand against it.

"Inside. Now." He'd spoken sharper than he intended, but couldn't take it back and inclined his head to the door.

She gave him a look. "Are you always this bossy?"

His smile happened before he could stop it. "You have no idea how bossy I can be, Toni."

She purred. "Hire me, Zach, and I will."

His smile died. "I can't."

"You won't."

Again, her response affirmed quiet resignation, not anger, which would have been easier for him to take.

She entered the diner.

Its beige-and-brown décor, along with wagon wheel light fixtures, fit the town's Old West theme. Even the souvenirs matched, Betty Boop and other cartoon characters dressed in a marketer's version of western wear.

Men of varying ages sat shoulder to shoulder on the few stools at the counter, their battered jeans, dusty cowboy boots, and Fruit of the Loom tees identifying them as locals. Tourists dressed in more colorful garb chattered at their Formica-and-chrome tables.

Emma Torres called out over the rising din, "Well, hey there!"

She stood near a table of elderly men from the retirement village. A hefty woman of thirty-five, Em liked her jeans tight, her checkered blouse snug, her brown hair worn short, and her pretty face scrubbed clean, no makeup. She waved at Zach wildly.

He grinned. Em and her husband Hector owned and operated this place.

As she worked her way past tables, she patted several women's shoulders, smiled at the men, and winked at the kids.

Upon reaching Zach, she pushed to her toes and pecked his cheek before giving a warm smile to Toni. "Be with you in a sec, hon. Soon as I seat him."

Zach cut in. "We're together."

Em's skinny eyebrows jumped up. "Table for two?"

He nodded. Her surprise wasn't any greater than his.

Em allowed herself a really good look at Toni, lingering on her leather pants and biker boots before glancing at the fringed saddlebag he carried. She gave him a loaded glance. "This way."

The booth she chose stood at the far end of the diner, away from the crowd. She rocked on her heels. "Best seat in the house."

It was certainly the most secluded. What did she think they planned to do back here? Hold hands? Whisper sweet nothings? Make out?

Toni stroked his fingers, her touch featherlight.

Sweet Jesus. He fought a pleasurable shiver until he noticed she wanted to take her saddlebag not flirt with him. Without too much delay, he gave it up.

She spoke to Em. "Where's the ladies' room?"

"Back there." She pointed. "Take an immediate left by the cash register and the souvenir stand."

"Thanks." Without a backward glance, Toni marched away.

With each step she took, her rounded cheeks bounced, begging for a man to hold them, delivering attention and satisfaction. To separate her succulent flesh then stroke her tight pink ring and lower, to her damp pussy.

Zach wiped his sweaty palms against his jeans.

Toni passed a table filled with elderly men. Several old guys turned in their chairs, following her with their eyes.

Once she'd rounded the corner and disappeared from view, Zach slid into his side of the booth. Harsh pain hit, traveling up his leg to his hip. He sucked in as much air as he could and tried to relax.

Em pretended she didn't see his agony. For that, he was grateful.

Rather than leave, as he wanted her to do, she plopped onto the padded seat across from him, clasped her hands on the table, and leaned forward. "Who is that?" She'd lowered her voice to a conspiratorial murmur. "Is she a tourist? Did you fix her car? Are you two going to be seeing each other?"

Zach propped his elbow on the table, his head in his palm.

"No, no, and no."

Her frown intensified the deep grooves above her nose. "What's that supposed to mean? You don't want to talk about it?"

Exactly. "There's nothing to talk about." He used his nicest tone. "I'm just answering your questions—no, no, and no."

"Wait a sec—what did I ask?"

He laughed.

"Now quit your teasing and dodging." She slapped his arm. "Who is she? And before you ask who I'm talking about, I mean that girl you came in with."

A huge mistake he hoped he wouldn't regret. He rubbed his forehead. "She's a mechanic."

Em's laughter rang louder than his. "On what planet?"

"She does seem to know about engines." Toni had surprised the hell out of him by picking the right tool and knowing a car actually had plugs.

She'd said Lucky had taught her.

Her smoky voice filled Zach's mind, thickening his blood, accelerating his heart, making him too curious again about who the fuck Lucky was and what else he had taught her. Like encouraging her to dress in toe to neck leather and wearing flowery perfume, a deceptively innocent scent.

"Hey." Em slapped his arm again. "I'm over here."

He turned from where Toni had gone, not realizing he'd been looking for her, and pretended nonchalance in spite of his hammering heart. "You haven't left yet?" He cocked one eyebrow. "Don't you have other guests to bother?"

"Nina can annoy them. How do you know she knows about engines?"

"Nina?"

Em gave him her mean look, the one she reserved for too rowdy diners. "The girl you brought in. What's her name?"

He grinned at how Toni had made him search for it. "It's

on the back of her jacket."

"Huh?"

"Starr." He liked testing the sound. "Toni Starr."

"Really. Sounds like a stripper."

He couldn't argue with that. "We talked shop back at the garage."

"She came by just to talk to you?"

"She wants a job."

"Oh." Em gave him a sly grin. "And you're going to—"

"No. I'm buying her breakfast, and then I'm giving her a few bucks so she can continue to eat while she looks for work."

"If she's that broke, why not hire her? From what I can see, you could use the help."

Zach readjusted his weight, making certain not to move his leg too much, and glanced past Em to the window. Tourists gathered near several shops to examine offered goods. Kids bounced next to their parents, either trying to get their attention or wanting to move on to someplace more interesting. "I have all the staff I need. I work on the vehicles after the guys go home."

"If you hired Ms. Starr, maybe you wouldn't have to work after hours. Maybe you could have a life."

He shot her a look.

She lifted her hands in surrender. "Just saying."

"I know, but I'm fine with the way things are."

"You mean hooking up with a woman, but only for the night."

Good God. "I am of age."

"Hell with that. You're lonely."

Better than being hurt again. "I am fine."

"No you're not. You keep to yourself too much. When you do go out with a woman, you don't keep her around for long. You dated the last one for what, a month? Even teens last longer with their girlfriends than you manage to do with yours. Now you listen to me . . ."

Having heard this before, he tuned her out. She made him sound like the town recluse the kids would someday whisper about, telling stories how he hid under automobiles to scare defenseless children.

Zach endured her lecture without comment.

Once she wound down, she offered a defeated sigh and slid out of her seat. "Guess I'm through here." She leaned toward him and spoke in a lowered voice not meant to be overheard. "Look out, here she comes."

Like Pavlov's dog hearing the bell, he glanced behind himself.

His heart stalled then picked up so much speed his throat constricted.

Toni had changed from her leather pants and biker boots to flip flops and black cut-off shorts. Several strings dangled down her milky thighs.

His cock stiffened.

Her feet were narrow, toes long, her nails polished a deep red. God help him, he wanted to kiss her sweet arch and touch the silver toe ring she wore on her right foot.

Before she reached their booth, he left his side and stood. Quick pain blasted him. He unclenched his jaw to hide his discomfort.

Toni's lips parted, concern on her face, telling him she'd noticed his agony.

"Well, hey there, welcome back!" Em's forced cheeriness pulled Toni's attention away from him. "Bet you're hungry." She grabbed two laminated menus from a wooden holder attached to the wall. "Here you go." She handed the first to Toni, the next to him.

"Thanks." Toni placed her saddlebag on her seat and slid in next to it.

Zach remained standing.

Looking like the third wheel at a blind date, Em stepped away from the booth. "Be back in a sec to take your orders."

He spoke before she could leave. "Bring some water right away. The whole pitcher, all right?"

Em snuck a look at Toni. "Sure. Coming right up."

Toni watched Em leave, then read the menu rather than observing him.

Thankful for her discretion, he took his seat.

She allowed him enough time to get comfortable then glanced up. "Whatever I want?"

For the first time in what seemed forever, he wanted to tease. "Within reason."

Toni leaned against the table. "Define reason."

He hadn't thought it possible, but her voice was throatier than he recalled, her guileless manner more provocative than the most blatant come-on. He had trouble pulling in a full breath. What little air he did manage to take in bore her unmistakable scent.

She must have sprayed more fragrance on her throat and wrists while she'd been in the ladies' room. Mixed with her inner heat, the scent brought to mind flowers caressed by the summer sun, mist rising from the fragrant earth, naked flesh stretched out on a blanket, tongues meeting, legs entwined, a cock nestled within a juicy, heated sheath.

She wanted him to define reason.

He hadn't an inkling what that might be. It sure as hell wasn't what happened to him whenever she was near. He knew he should get a grip and treat her like the stranger she was, yet couldn't. "Where are you from?" He hadn't meant to blurt such a personal question but needed to know. "Originally?"

A long moment passed before she lowered her menu to the table. "Why?" She forced the sudden caution off her face, replacing it with a lazy smile. "You worried I don't have a Social Security number? That I'm not authorized to work in this country?"

He almost smiled at her tenacity in wanting a job. But only for a month, she'd said. Four short weeks so she could spring her bike from impound and zoom away never to be seen again. As it should be. So why did that disturb him? "Just curious, that's all."

Her eyes and face hid whatever she thought. "I'm from a lot of places."

He waited for her to add details, even though he figured she wouldn't. He warned himself not to stare but failed, taking in her hair skimming her slender throat, the hollow between her breasts, her erect nipples pushing against her top, the hard buds reacting to chilled air pouring from the vent above them.

She leaned back in her seat and glanced past, her mood unreadable. "I want that."

Longing sounded in her voice.

Curious as to why, he followed her gaze to a nearby table, the young man, woman, and two preschool children seated there. Their blond good looks and innocent smiles made them a Norman Rockwell portrait of the perfect family from the fifties. Zach didn't understand why she was looking at them. "You want what?"

She lowered her face. "I haven't had whipped cream on waffles in a long time."

The woman's plate held the sweet treat.

"I'd also like what the guy's eating." She shrugged. "His omelet looks really good."

Despite her cavalier gesture, she sounded like most women would when viewing diamonds or precious gems rather than ordinary food. *What in the world have you been through?* No one in this damn country should go hungry. Pained at what she lacked, he spoke as gently as he could. "Get whatever you want."

She lifted her face, yearning in her eyes, followed by naked and wanting desire.

His heart made a weird twist. He couldn't glance away.

She wore the look a woman does when she'd allow a man anything and would willingly explore his and her needs wherever he demanded.

Intense warmth settled in his chest and throat. His scalp tingled.

Toni crossed her legs. Her foot brushed his calf and remained there. He didn't move his leg either. Their gazes remained locked. Silence embraced them, feeling somehow right, while the restaurant hummed with activity and sound. Johnny Cash sang *Ring of Fire,* the air-conditioning system whooshed out cold air, utensils clacked against plates, people gabbed and laughed.

Em delivered the pitcher he'd asked for. "Have you two decided yet?"

Zach poured ice water into a glass and pushed it to Toni's side. "Ladies first."

Her cheeks pinked up.

Em tapped her pen against her pad. "So, what do you want, hon?"

Toni glanced at the menu, then looked at Em. "A job. I'll waitress or wash dishes or clean the place. Your choice."

Em looked at Zach.

So did Toni. "Oh crud." Dismay filled her face and voice. "Do you own this place, too?"

Em laughed. "No, hon. I own it with my husband, Hector. He's the cook."

Toni brightened. "I can help him."

Zach stared. She couldn't be a short-order cook, too, though with her anything was possible. "I thought you were a mechanic, at least when you're not being a daredevil."

Em frowned. "A what?"

Toni spoke to him. "I'm a mechanic and a motorcycle performance artist, when I'm employed." She focused on Em. "I'm not saying I can cook, but I can follow a recipe. It's not rocket science, right?"

Em rested her hand on her ample hip. The lines above her nose got seriously nasty with her frown. "To Hector, it is. He's very proud of what he does."

"I won't screw it up, I swear." Toni grinned so hard her cheeks must have hurt. "All I want is a chance to earn some money." She craned her neck. "Is that Hector?" She pointed across the room to the rectangular window that revealed the kitchen. Hector, swarthy and sweating, alternately cooked and directed the younger man at his side. "Maybe we can talk."

"I don't think so." Em didn't move, which effectively blocked Toni from leaving her seat. "Like Zach said, you're a mechanic. Better stick with what you know."

"Even if it means I'll starve? Look, it's only for a month until I can make enough to get my bike out of prison."

Em made a face. "Outta where?"

Zach rubbed his temple. "It's a long story."

Toni hung her head.

His stomach clenched at her desperation. Tenderness flooded him before he could stop the emotion. She walked a fair piece today before reaching Indulgence and had accepted a ride from a stranger who could have been a rapist or psychopath. Why hadn't she cared about her safety? Were such concerns only for young women who had families that cared and had money to protect them from harm?

Toni scooted closer to Em. "Please, I'll do whatever odd jobs you have around here. I'll—"

Zach cut in. "A month, no more than that."

" — work hard — what?" Toni looked at him.

He pushed his paper napkin and utensils to the right then back to the left. "I'll give you a month at my place. Standard wage."

Her eyes rounded in surprise. A smile blossomed across her face.

Her joy was so luminous and breathtakingly happy, he barely caught himself from returning her smile.

"How standard for the wage?" She pointed at him, pure sass now. "Same as the guys?"

God, he liked her style but wasn't about to show it. Acting as a boss should, he affected his steeliest look and crossed his arms.

She grinned. "Better than the guys?"

Em chuckled. "If he's wise."

Zach stared at her then Toni.

Partly deflated, Toni searched his face. "You're sure about this? Me working with you?"

He thought it was *for* him, and hell no, he wasn't certain about anything, but he was a man of his word. He'd help her for a month, then see her on her way. Out of his life and thoughts. He'd give her a kiss goodbye for luck.

He'd hug her so hard she'd lose her breath and whatever resistance she might have had. He'd capture her mouth and plunge his tongue inside, his kiss uncivilized, impatient for more. He'd tunnel his hand beneath her top and free her breast from her bra, cradle her naked flesh in his palm, test its precious weight, then know emptiness and coldness once she was gone.

Which she would be in a month. Going back to wherever she'd come from. Maybe a place she'd escaped. When women were alone like she was, without friends or family to help, most likely an SOB was involved.

A man she might have loved.

Surprising and intense jealousy hit him.

"Zach?" Toni looked at him questioningly.

He finished half her water and wiped his mouth with the back of his hand. "Yeah, I'm sure."

CHAPTER FOUR

Twenty minutes before her shift ended, Toni finished balancing and rotating the tires on a Ford Ranger. Its owner, a forty-something guy with receding red hair, watched her from the open bay doors.

Feeling frisky, she gave him two thumbs up.

His face flushed, matching the reddish freckles on his scalp. He lowered his soda. "You're done?"

She flicked the rack switch to lower his pickup to the floor. "Will be in a sec. Soon as I settle the paperwork."

He exchanged a glance with the guys crowded next to him, who'd also watched her. As one, they clapped in wild applause. The youngest in the group offered a celebratory whistle.

Grinning, Toni bowed from the waist, playing into their teasing, liking the camaraderie. It reminded her of the good times she'd had with Lucky and Belle.

Several days ago, she'd literally spent her last dimes and quarters to call them. Not to inform them about her arrest and losing her bike, but to lie and assure them she was okay.

She was for the time being. With the money she'd make from this gig, she'd be able to send them some funds then get her bike from impound and spring for cheapo insurance. After that, she'd have to be on her way.

Zach had warned she had no more than a month here.

The applause died down, and so did her smile.

Her first day here was almost gone, passing with surprising speed, reminding her of a life she hadn't experienced in too long. One offering stability and knowing what the next day would bring. Throughout the morning and afternoon, she'd been able to relax even though the locals kept stopping by to observe the female mechanic, a curiosity apparently unheard of in Indulgence.

The younger guys grinned openly as if she were slithering down a pole in an X-rated nightclub rather than wearing baggy blue overalls — the same as Robbie and Angel, the other mechanic.

All through the day, she'd felt Zach watching her. When she'd glanced at his office, he hadn't averted his gaze or ducked away from the window to return to his desk. He'd regarded her with the same intensity as the moment they met.

Ignoring him proved impossible.

Too quickly, she'd become wanting: desiring his touch, hearing his rich baritone, witnessing the pleasure in his smile because of something she'd said. At this rate, leaving here and never seeing him again, would be damn difficult, but necessary. He'd given her four weeks. Better than she'd hoped for.

She finished her paperwork and crossed the work area to his office, her biker boots tapping sharply against the concrete floor.

Zach glanced from the middle-aged woman he was speaking with, to her.

"Sorry to interrupt." Toni lifted the clipboard to show him why she was here.

He reached for the paperwork. "Is this the Miller work order?"

She nodded.

He took the clipboard, his fingers touching hers, lingering on them.

Her legs went watery, her mouth dry. Despite cold air pouring from the ceiling vents, she'd never been as hot.

"Thanks." He laid the paperwork on his desk.

Back in the garage, the oppressive heat and Faith Hill singing on the radio finally bled into Toni's consciousness. Her hands shook as she put away the tools. Partly due to her reaction to Zach. Also because the day was ending, the night looming.

She pivoted and flinched at Robbie and Angel standing so close, their tools in hand.

No one stood at the bay doors, the customers and gawkers having drifted away while she'd been in deep lust over Zach and worry about this evening.

She backed up and gave the guys a smile. "Sorry, didn't mean to get in your way."

Angel spoke first. "You didn't—you're not." He proved as hefty as Robbie was skinny. In addition to a shaved head, Angel sported a dream catcher tattoo on his thick neck and an ornate cross tat on his meaty wrist. "We . . . Robbie and me . . . were wondering what you planned to do tonight."

Good question. Luckily, she'd had an enormous breakfast and lunch, thanks to Zach, with him ordering pizza for the entire crew. Given the guys' surprised expressions, she suspected Zach's generosity wasn't typical.

At least she wouldn't go hungry tonight. As to where she planned to stay . . .

Robbie grinned. "Are you up for some fun?"

Entertainment cost money she didn't have. Even one beer wasn't possible, the same as hanging out with these guys. They were sweet as could be, but she couldn't expect them to pay for anything, nor could she ask to crash at their places, no matter her situation. She didn't want Zach thinking she might be sleeping with his employees in exchange for a bed.

With a negligent shrug, she put on her tough-girl act, one she'd perfected over the years. "I think I'm going to crash. Been a busy day, you know?"

"Oh sure." Angel held up his hands. "I hear you."

Robbie scratched his shoulder. "Where you staying?"

Another good question she had no answer for unless she lied. "This place at the edge of town. Nothing fancy."

"An apartment?" Robbie's thin face glowed with curiosity. "The Phoenix complex on Cottonwood Avenue or the—"

Zach cut in. "You guys done for the day?" He regarded the younger men, then her, his stance territorial, befitting a male in his prime.

The air between them seemed to crackle with promise.

Every part of her hummed with desire.

Robbie put his tools in the chest. "Just getting ready to clock out."

Angel leaned toward her and spoke quietly. "We can all do something tomorrow."

He and Robbie made quick work cleaning up and stripping from their overalls to their street clothes.

Toni raised her hand in farewell to them, then lingered by the tool cabinet, taking her time putting things away.

At last the garage was empty except for her and Zach. Her heart beat too fast. Taking a full breath became increasingly difficult. She felt awkward suddenly, not knowing what to say or to do.

She knew what she wanted: Zach to touch her, hold her, give her a sense of belonging if only for the night. To love her in his bed hard and long, easing her intolerable loneliness with physical and emotional contact, warmth and tenderness. She suspected he wanted the same, at least as far as the sex went. Even so, she had to take care not to cross an invisible line between employee and boss, which might risk her job. That meant letting him make the first move.

He joined her at the cabinet and leaned against it.

Their arms were inches apart. Anticipation and pleasure rolled through her.

He stroked the cabinet.

The glide registered in her pussy.

"How'd it go today?"

His voice was softer than usual, a balm for her bruised soul. She wanted to be straight with him and confess her secrets, ask for his comfort and understanding but knew that wasn't possible. He was being kind not asking them to be BFFs. "Better than you expected?"

He laughed. "You do good work."

Surprise and gratitude rushed through her. His praise meant more than he would ever know, comforting her as no food or drink could. She recalled her father's approval, still missing him terribly after so many years. A dull ache swept across her chest. She willed it away, reluctant to allow sweet memories with her dad to bring back the bad ones she'd buried for too long. What she had now, right this minute, would have to be enough. Pushing back sentimentality, she looked down her nose at Zach. "Yeah, I know."

His smile brightened at her bravado, then fled with his questioning look. "So, what now?" He regarded her grease-and-oil-stained overalls.

Uncertain as to what he meant, and not wanting to ruin anything in case she'd read him wrong, she kept joking around. "You pay me for a day's work? While you head out, I clean up in here and see you in the morning?"

"Where are you planning on staying tonight?" He regarded her carefully, his mood solemn. "Were you thinking of crashing in my office?"

Heat surged to her throat and face at him guessing her plan. He had a reasonably comfortable sofa in there that looked as if he'd spent more than a few nights on it. "I won't take anything." Embarrassment and desperation laced her promise. "I'm not a thief."

Concern swept his features. "No one said you are." He pushed away from the cabinet and flipped the controls for the bay doors. "Finish up." He spoke loud enough so she could hear him over the rattling metal. "Then come into my office."

He left.

Her heart beat painfully in hope that he'd let her stay in there and also worry he'd changed his mind about her employment, intending to terminate her because she was still a stranger and a possible thief. She cursed her big mouth. "Why?"

He stopped and looked over. The doors reached the floor, thwacking it. "So I can take you home."

She wasn't following. "What?"

He faced her. "You don't have any money to spend on a motel room and you've already said you won't be going back to the shelter. So I'm offering you a place to stay."

She still didn't understand. "With who?"

His gaze roamed her, renewed intensity in his eyes. "Me."

Her heart stumbled on several beats, muddying her thoughts, denying her breath.

Their silence lengthened

His demeanor shifted back to the forced restraint he'd shown earlier. "Don't worry. I know how to handle myself." He reached his office.

Without thinking, she called out, "I know that." She could see and hear it.

Once more, he looked over.

God, you're something. Not only hot but too kind and honorable to take advantage of a woman. "I'm not worried."

Something dark and dangerous flared in his eyes, telling her she *should* take care. He wasn't a man to toy with. If a woman desired him, he'd enjoy her any way he chose, and once he started, nothing would stop him. He'd take what he wanted while providing equal pleasure.

Her legs weakened. She leaned against the cabinet, needing the support.

"Don't make me wait." Domination and pleasure played in

his voice. Not giving her a chance to respond, he entered his office.

Seconds later, something banged then rattled against a metal cabinet.

She guessed he'd tossed a clipboard there.

The air-conditioning shut off.

She tried to picture his place, a one-bedroom apartment surely, just large enough for two. He'd either tell her to sleep on the sofa or might offer her his bed. They'd possibly talk before going to sleep, watch TV, share a drink or dinner.

During the night, would he lose control and join her, trapping her with his big body, one hand holding her wrists above her head while his other roamed?

Her lids slid down. Images flashed in her mind: his rigid cock pressed against her mound, him pulling her top and bra off to bare her breasts, lowering his mouth to them, pulling her stiffened nipples inside.

Her pussy creamed.

His lips would be heated and soft on her, his bristly cheeks scraping her breasts.

In a perfect world, he'd take her with passion and need, wanting no woman except her. An outrageous fantasy she shouldn't indulge in.

Had he ever loved anyone?

Even if he had, she sensed he didn't now. He wouldn't be bringing her to his home or offering her a place to sleep if he had a girlfriend he cared about. He wouldn't be crossing the fragile line separating employer from employee, man from woman, stranger from lover.

He wouldn't be telling her not to make him wait as carnal promise sparked in his eyes.

Once Toni had buckled herself in Zach's black Ram, he eased his pickup through the town's historic section, picking up speed as he reached the newer area. Unable to manage small talk, she waited for him to say something.

He didn't, listening instead to a Garth Brooks song on the radio. Or maybe he was lost in thought, wondering why he'd offered her shelter for the night.

And not in any apartment.

He kept passing the few complexes dotting the landscape.

A retirement village came next, followed by a new housing development and a strip mall, boasting a convenience store and beauty parlor called Pat's Place. Beyond it, open country spread in every direction. Towering trees crowded together in clumps, their branches thick with leaves that reached the ground. Gentle hills tinted a dark rose peeked from above the foliage, their mild contours dotted with thirsty-looking shrubs and cacti.

Since the scenery gave her nothing to go on, she had to make an educated guess. "You live in a trailer?"

Zach turned down the volume on Keith Urban's song and looked over. "Nope."

She hazarded another guess. "A tent?"

Smiling, he pointed. "Up ahead."

Several billboards hawked animal feed, liquor, and real estate for sale. That one displayed the realtor's photo next to a two-story Victorian. Past it, a paved road snaked off the main one before disappearing within the trees. "You have a log cabin?"

"Not even close." He slowed his pickup and made a right on the road.

Branches canopied the drive that continued up a meek hill. The trees thinned out at the top to reveal an expansive front yard with bright green grass, colorful flower beds, and the beige-and-white Victorian from the billboard, the house likely historic and lovingly restored.

White gingerbread graced the overhang on the wide porch

and the inverted V on the roof. A beige gas lamp sporting four white globes stood sentinel near the front steps. At two stories, the place had to have at least three bedrooms.

Lacy white curtains adorned the spotless windows on the room at the top. The perfect place for a beloved little girl.

He couldn't have children.

Afraid to ask, she tried not to stare at the house but couldn't help herself, loving its beauty, uniqueness, and welcoming feel that offered its owner comfort and sanctuary from a heartless world.

Though maybe not for him. A 'for sale' sign hung from the porch rail to the left. Placed there in case someone missed the billboard?

"You're selling your house, huh?" She gestured to the sign. "This is your house, right?"

"Yep." He parked in the shade and turned off the engine. "I've been trying to get rid of it for nearly a year. In this area's crappy economy, there haven't been any takers." He popped his door, rounded the vehicle to her side, and offered his hand to help her out.

She hauled her saddlebag off the cab floor. "Thanks." She slipped her fingers over his.

His warm, dry palm electrified, leaving her breathless and weak. His gentle strength made her feel fragile and clumsy at the same time.

The moment her feet hit the ground, any other guy in his position would have released her. Zach didn't. They stared at each other. She curled her fingers over his.

Desire burned in his eyes.

Her pulse thudded. She eased closer.

Numerous birds squawked from the overhead tree and took wing.

He brought back his hand and leaned into the cab, collecting her jacket and helmet.

His ass was delightfully tight, his thighs powerful. Her own tensed with need.

He straightened.

Pretending nonchalance, she opted for chitchat. "Did you buy this place as an investment?"

He draped her jacket over his arm, propped her helmet beneath it, then inclined his head to the house. "This way."

Lemon furniture polish scented the small foyer, along with a faint bacon aroma. The hardwood floors gleamed, reflecting everything in their path. White wainscoting paneled the pale yellow walls. Antique-looking chairs with needlepoint backs and seats flanked a mahogany accent table. On it stood a brass lamp with a gold-fringed shade. Landscapes painted in delicate pastels rounded out the lovely and surprising décor.

He had to be divorced. She guessed before his marriage went south, his ex-wife had decorated this place. He didn't seem the type to ponder fabrics, paint, and furniture, or consult with a decorator. Why his ex would have allowed him to keep their home in the settlement mystified Toni.

Zach left the foyer and stopped at the stairway.

Dutifully, she followed, but couldn't help but snoop. A room to the left was a formal living room, complete with a stone fireplace and Victorian-style furniture upholstered in rose brocade that matched the wall color.

Wow.

Overwhelmed, she reached him. "This is a really nice place."

He gave her an amused smile. "Want to buy it?"

"Give me a raise, and I'll consider your offer."

He wagged his finger then climbed the stairs, leading her down a narrow hall to the first door on the right. There, he stopped and gestured her inside.

She stopped smack in the center, too captivated to take another step. A brass queen-sized bed dominated the snug space, its crocheted comforter and pillow shams an ecru shade dotted with pink rosettes. Gauzy ivory curtains embellished the tall window. A dressing table with a circular mirror graced the wall to the right. To the left stood a display case holding numerous dolls in vintage clothes identical to the little girl in that ancient movie *Pollyanna*.

Memories bore down on Toni, along with such fierce longing her shoulders and stomach ached. She recalled her childhood when she had a bedroom as feminine and welcoming . . . as safe as this one, the comfort in her father's arms surrounding her, him saying she was precious, wanted, welcomed, loved. He'd always be there to protect her.

She could still taste the hopelessness she'd experienced when he died.

Zach entered the room, the wood floor groaning beneath his weight.

She turned away and blinked repeatedly to clear her eyes, not wanting him to witness her sorrow.

He made an indistinct sound. "Is the room all right?"

She pushed emotion and yearning for the past from her heart. "It's beautiful." She lowered her saddlebag to the floor near the bed and touched a rosette, determined to concentrate on the present. "You live here alone?"

He draped her jacket over the brass baseboard, put her helmet on the mattress, and backed to the door. "The bath's in the hall. Everything you need is in there."

How wrong he was. She needed too many years back, a place to call home, and if she were very lucky, a guy like Zach. Defenseless against her thoughts and his allure, she faced him.

He regarded her, a questioning look in his eyes.

Please don't ask me anything I can't answer.

For her, it was less painful to keep their relationship casual and purely physical, if things evolved to that. She couldn't deny her hope for as much and ran her thumbnail down her cut-offs, barely able to hide her arousal, her desire for contact no matter how brief.

He stared at her legs. "I was going to grill steaks for dinner. That okay with you?"

For the first time in years, food wasn't what she wanted more than anything else. She sensed he didn't crave it either. Even so, it was his home and his call as to what they did. "Sounds good." She joined him, close enough for them to touch. "Anything I can do?"

He glanced past her to the bed, his face distracted and wanting. Too quickly, he looked over at the hall. "Get settled." His shoulders were tight, his voice strained. "Freshen up if you want. I'll see you downstairs."

He left.

Slumped against the fridge, Zach tilted his head back and gulped his Coors. Above him, water pounded in the tub from Toni's shower. His attention drifted to the ceiling. Provocative and tempting pictures rose in his mind: Toni stripping off her stretchy top and bra, her full breasts bouncing prettily, the cut-off strings dangling over her knees and calves as she pushed the shorts down then stepped out of them and what he guessed — or hoped — was her thong.

With her pale flesh bared, the only color would be her rosy nipples, the dark curls between her legs, and her polished toenails. Did she bathe with her toe ring on?

Maybe.

Perspiration rolled from his neck to his chest.

A pipe rattled.

He pressed the chilled bottle to his forehead, much as she'd done with the water he'd given her this morning.

Those moments seemed a lifetime away. Like she'd always been working with him and spending the night here.

She wanted to know if he lived alone.

For almost two years. Not that those days had been anything close to a normal existence. More like getting through each second, minute, and hour. He ate, worked, and slept, period, except for his occasional dates with women he liked but could never love. Breaking up with them after a few weeks or months was kinder than stringing them along.

No one, especially Em, had to tell Zach he feared risking his heart again and because he did he'd held onto this place for too long, as if keeping it would change the past. It couldn't, of course. No more than he could flap his arms and fly.

And now Toni was here, at least for a short while.

He needed to know where she hailed from and where she'd go once she left Indulgence. When she'd glanced around the bedroom, intense yearning tightened her features, stunning him to silence. She looked as though she'd never slept in such a nice place.

Meg had decorated their home as a bed-and-breakfast she never got a chance to open. Because of him. One stupid, fucking, lousy decision he'd made had taken her life, and he couldn't make things better and bring her back. Hell, he hadn't even been able to apologize. She was gone before he could.

The water shut off and the pipes banged in momentary protest.

Edgy yet exhausted, he rubbed his eyes, relieved Toni would only be here for a month. Yet, he also considered how empty this house and his garage would be without her.

Guilt sliced through him, followed by wrenching desire.

He was losing his goddamn mind.

On a muttered curse, he ordered himself to shake off his feelings, get through this night and the others. After finishing his beer, he pushed away from the fridge to prepare their meal.

Toni stopped at the bottom of the stairs, not knowing where to find Zach. She located the formal dining room, liking its quaint beauty, but he wasn't inside. After traversing a narrow hall, she ended up in the surprisingly large kitchen equipped with new copper-colored appliances and wooden cabinets in a honey color.

This room was also empty.

She put her hand on the stove to check its heat even though she figured he hadn't turned it on. The room was too cool. The microwave on the rust-colored countertop wasn't cooking anything.

Wait — he'd talked about grilling steaks. *Outside?*

She eased the lacy curtain from the backdoor window, revealing an expansive yard, a pool, brick barbecue, and Zach. Reckless longing for his presence, conversation, and the chance to get to know him sped through her, making her dizzy. She seized the opportunity to at least ogle him as much as she wanted. The same as this morning before she'd approached his garage.

As he shook charcoal from a large bag, his pecs and biceps flexed. She sucked her bottom lip. A slight breeze lifted the locks dangling over his forehead. His lashes were sooty, eyes surprisingly light against them, his stubble drool worthy.

Damn, you're gorgeous. So damn virile and, more importantly, decent he stole her breath and allowed her to imagine what her future could have been if Joe hadn't come into her life. How he'd changed everyt0hing, leading her to work on the circuit, the only thing she knew, rather than coming home to a man like Zach every night. She pictured them laughing or bitching about their respective careers, showering together, washing off grime and whatever frustrations they'd faced. Lovingly, she'd tend to him, from head to toes. On her knees, she'd wash his balls and cock, pressing her face into his thick, dark curls, licking moisture from them and his rigid shaft. In bed they'd feast on each other's nudity, restoring comfort and peace before their meal.

Some days they might forget to eat, too exhausted from working diligently and loving even harder to bother.

Foolish tears crowded her eyes.

Zach looked over, catching her staring at him.

His attention sapped her strength and will to resist another moment apart. Once she dried her eyes, she joined him on the patio. With the lowering sun, the heated air had transformed from unbearable to temptingly soft. Long shadows flowed from the vegetation on the surrounding hills. Startling quiet surrounded them, noise from vehicles, people, and civilization gone.

Blood rushed in her ears. Doing her best to behave casually, she took in the barbecue rather than him. "Smells good."

"I haven't cooked anything yet. I just lit the grill."

She gave him an agreeable smile.

He regarded her hot pink tank top and white cut-offs, the best clothes she had outside of her leather pants and jacket. Given the way he stared, he approved.

Buoyed by his response when she shouldn't have been, given their tentative relationship, she tried not to focus on him and failed. His arms were sinewy, hands large, fingers long. The thick ridge behind his fly drew her as nothing else could. "Are you divorced?"

Caution then irritation registered in his eyes. He glanced past her to the cedar picnic table. Sirloins, ears of corn, and foil wrapped potatoes rested on a tray. "I'm not married if that's what you want to know. How about you?"

She chided herself for asking him anything personal. "Never been close."

"So, Lucky's not an ex-husband? He's an ex-boyfriend you've been running from?"

An inner alarm warned her to dodge his questions. One always led to too many, which she wouldn't be willing to answer. Yet, something inside urged her to respond truthfully, to share some history with him, as if they did live here together, rather than her being a barely invited guest. "I'd never run from Lucky or Belle."

Curiosity shone in Zach's eyes. "Belle?"

"My people." She shrugged. "My family."

He looked confused. "You mean your mom and dad?"

"Here." She reached beneath her tank top and into her bra cup.

Zach hadn't a clue what she was doing. Before he could ask, she pulled out a small laminated piece, the size of a driver's license, and offered it to him.

Her freshly washed hair bore the same scent as her perfume, the fragrance surrounding and embracing him.

He had to lock his knees to keep steady and endure the gnawing pain that caused his leg. Her body heat had warmed the plastic. Fighting an insane urge to press it to his nose to see if it also bore her scent, he treated the piece with respect, because it was important to her.

The picture showed a man and woman, arms draped around each other's waists. He guessed them to be in their early fifties.

The man — had to be Lucky — had long brown hair streaked with gray that he wore in braids, ala Willie Nelson. Belle's auburn hair hung over her right shoulder, the ends reaching her waist. Her lingering beauty told Zach she must have been a babe when she'd been young. Lucky's muscular build and broad smile made him a handsome man.

Both wore turquoise-and-silver Indian jewelry. They stood by numerous motorcycles. Behind them, the storefront sign read Starr's Shop.

He checked their features against Toni's and saw zero resemblance despite them sharing the same last name. To his surprise, it was real enough to put on a shop. "Your parents?"

"My family." Toni reached for the photo. "I adopted them."

Her strange answer surprised him. Maybe she was as unglued around him as he was with her and couldn't think straight. "You mean they adopted you?"

She took the picture, giving him no answer as he'd often done with her.

What a pair they made. He wondered what kind of loneliness would cause a woman to carry a photo close to her heart of two people who weren't even related to her. "Where are they? Where do they live?"

She slipped the picture back into her bra and adjusted her tank top. "Arkansas."

Another surprise since he'd expected her to say Texas. On her job app, she'd listed a town there he'd never heard of and general delivery as her home address. "If they're in Arkansas with their own shop, what are you doing in Arizona looking for work?"

"Nice pool." She fled him and reached the deep end in record speed. "Mind if I put my feet in the water?"

"Of course not. Go ahead."

She kicked off her flip flops, sank to her ass, and dangled her legs in the water. "Mmm." She lifted her chin to the sky. "Nice."

Her throaty voice and that near purr drove away his next questions. Desire licked his groin and scattered his thoughts, until the breeze delivered smoking charcoal to him. Remembering their meal, he placed the already baked potatoes on the grill to heat them up, then tended the corn.

She made no sounds, not even a pleased sigh. Her hair, still damp from the shower, clung to her pale neck.

Without warning, she looked over, catching him staring.

He wasn't about to apologize.

Her softened features and parted lips said she didn't want one. "It's new."

Not following, he shook his head. "What's new?"

"Belle and Lucky's shop." She spoke on a sigh, her voice relaxed, smoky and sensuous. "They can barely pay themselves, much less me." She lifted her right leg from the water.

Droplets sparkled on her narrow foot and slender toes. Her polished toenails and silver ring gave him a quick hard-on that became painful fast. He wanted to slip the jewelry off, stripping her completely bare, then enjoy her pale, naked flesh beneath his.

"When I can."

He should have been listening to what she'd said. Too late now. "Sorry, I didn't catch that. When you can what?"

She lowered her leg into the water then lifted her other foot and splayed her toes. "I send Belle and Lucky money when I can." She looked at her foot rather than him. "I'll be able to really help out when I return to the circuit a month from now."

He frowned when he shouldn't have, but couldn't help the stunning and ruthless possessiveness gripping him concerning her expected departure.

She should be on her way in a month. Hell, she shouldn't be here at all. Giving her a job and a place to stay had been a huge mistake. She wasn't his to care about. They'd never be anything more to each other than what they were at this moment—employee and boss, polite acquaintances, lasting strangers.

No way would he allow anything else.

Chapter Five

For Toni, her and Zach's second meal together was definitely different than their first, though not better. At the diner, they'd at least touched accidentally or, in her case, accidentally on purpose, and discussed her work at his place.

At the cedar table, he plied her with personal questions. "What cities have you been to?"

She buttered and salted her corn. "Too many to count. Mostly small. No one's ever heard of them."

"Try me."

Challenged, she named the smallest she could remember.

Each drew a blank from him. He didn't give up. "Where do your friends live?"

She hadn't had any lasting ones since high school. She'd been on the move too much. "All over."

"Where'd you go to school?"

Her stomach fell. She forced a smile. "Afraid I didn't get a diploma because I'm merely a motorcycle performance artist and a sometime mechanic?"

Embarrassment flooded his face. "No. I didn't mean anything. I—tell me about Lucky and Belle's shop."

She gushed about it, embellishing their inventory, telling him how excited they were to have the place up and running. It had always been their dream. "Once it's a success, I can help out. Lucky taught me everything I know. He can repair any vehicle."

"Such as?"

She detailed his talents and what she'd learned, easy stuff

to talk about.

Zach listened without interruption, challenge, or more pointed questions.

After she said all she could, they again fell to silence like couples everywhere else, keeping to themselves as they ate their meal. Unable to withstand the increasingly strained mood, she prompted him to discuss work at the garage, a safe subject. "So are you paying me more than the guys?"

He swiped a napkin over his mouth.

Too bad. She would have liked to lick the butter from his lips then let him taste her every-freaking-where. "Is that a yes?"

He sniffed. "You wish."

Hmm. "About that Caddy the older woman brought in . . ."

They discussed its problems, which included the air-conditioning system.

Zach took the pepper from Toni's side. "No matter what it needs, the owner doesn't want a huge expense."

"If she doesn't get it fixed, she'll die from the heat. Then you'll be up for manslaughter."

"Me?" He put down the pepper. "You're the one doing the work."

She pushed out her bottom lip. "Would you actually throw me under the bus?"

He worked his mouth to hide his smile, then pointed to her corn and potato. "Eat your vegetables."

His command wasn't exactly sultry BDSM talk from a Master, but she liked that he was looking out for her.

Once they exhausted cars, they discussed the crappy economy, the continuing decline in real estate, with him doing most of the whining, and every issue imaginable as long as it didn't include anything personal.

In a beautiful setting accompanied by a soft breeze, good food, and intensifying lust, they behaved like an old married couple burned by too much intimacy.

There wasn't anything she could do to change things since she wasn't willing to open her past to him. If he'd wanted to do so with her, she would have listened clear to next month and beyond.

He offered nothing.

Afraid they'd lapsed into another silent interlude, she bitched about the networks' stupid reality shows. "Seriously, I know the Kardashians and other celebs are popular, but tuning into their lives is like watching people try to get out of jury duty—occasional hysterics with long stretches of pure boredom."

His shoulders bobbed with laughter. "They're not my favorite."

"Wow. You actually watch them?"

"I did a drive by once. Don't you dare tell anyone."

"Give me a raise, and I'll think about it."

He finished his potato. "A raise? On your first day?"

"Sure."

"You're lucky I don't dock you for drawing a crowd."

She leaned toward him. "You should charge the gawkers to watch me."

"There's a thought." He licked his fork. Sour cream lingered on his bottom lip.

She wiped it off and sucked the condiment from her finger. Only then did she realize what she'd done and so effortlessly, too.

His color heightened.

Her face felt as if it were on fire.

Imprisoned in the moment, they stared, the same as numerous times today in the garage and at the diner. Brute lust and animal need flooded his face.

Her heart thudded. Not daring to take a breath, she waited for him to haul her close for a merciless kiss, to acknowledge their hunger for each other.

Seconds dragged by.

He looked away.

She slumped then swung her legs over the bench and stood, her insides still trembling from desire. "How about a swim? That stuff about drowning after eating is bull. I know. I've tempted fate dozens of times and I'm still breathing. Come on."

He fingered his beer bottle. "No. You go ahead."

"You don't like to swim?"

"I have to clean up."

"I'll help."

"No. Swim. Go to bed. Watch TV. Read a book." He stacked plates. "I'll do this myself."

Afraid to piss him off further, she backed away. "I think I'll crash. Have a nice night."

She ran to her bedroom, praying he'd follow.

He didn't.

For hours, she slept fitfully and now stared into darkness, figuring it must be late. Even the boisterous crickets had settled down, bringing unwelcomed quiet.

Naked, she pushed the top sheet to the baseboard and tried not to focus on Zach in his bedroom down the hall. Needing something to calm down, she stroked her swollen and damp folds and rubbed her clit.

Delight and warmth spread to her belly and down her thighs. Her breath caught.

Zach invaded her mind.

Don't go there.

She tried to push his image away along with his remembered scent and touch, but couldn't. His laughter warmed her soul. His smile made the day worthwhile. His kindness was too wonderful for words. His wicked teasing the best.

Her orgasm neared.

She rubbed her clit fast and hard. Too quickly, she

climaxed, and pleasure died, not coming close to sating the emptiness inside her life, heart, and body.

With his arm draped over his forehead and his fist clenched, Zach regarded the fading shadows on the master bedroom ceiling.

It couldn't be time to get up.

According to the clock, he had ten minutes before the alarm went off.

Fuck. He'd barely slept.

Each time he'd managed to drift off, he'd awakened in a start from dreams he couldn't recall. Tension knotted his neck and shoulders. His arms and legs refused to relax. An hour ago, he'd finally given in and masturbated like an out-of-control teen, releasing his cum on his belly rather than in a warm, soft female.

Toni.

Uh-uh. No damn way. Even if she did stir him as few females had, she was a complication he didn't need.

He rolled onto his belly. Instantly, his knee and leg hurt. He sucked air and squeezed his lids.

Toni's image arrived without pause, the way she'd looked outside during dinner, her hair swinging against her smooth cheeks, plump lower lip shiny from the steak, eyes searching his, her mood wanting and receptive.

If he'd taken her on the picnic table, he figured she wouldn't have protested. Hell, she probably would have encouraged it and more . . . a lot more. Anything he wanted, no matter how crazy or lewd.

Like tying her wrists to the bed and playing pirate or whatever the hell women fantasized about. Having her willingly submit to his dominance and beg for more, playing those games in fun and for mutual pleasure.

Unlike Meg, Toni hadn't been sheltered. She behaved as if she expected such behavior from a man, practically coaxing it from him. Yet, despite her gutsy personality and the brave front she kept putting on, she had a world-weariness about her, a forlornness that kept pulling him near. Telling him he could ease whatever hurt she'd known, past or present. They could comfort each other.

Until she left, and she would. She had Lucky and Belle to support.

He couldn't figure out who in the fuck they were, where in the hell she'd met them, or what it meant that she'd adopted them, rather than they'd done so with her.

At dinner last night, she'd piled on the praise for Belle and Lucky, but offered nothing truly personal about them, including what their previous jobs had been.

He hadn't dared ask. Instead, he'd let her talk. Her love for the couple transformed and relaxed her, allowing Toni to smile freely, laugh recklessly, turning her into one of the most interesting and surely most desirable women he'd ever known.

And he didn't know her at all.

Today certainly wouldn't change that. He turned to the clock.

Shit. Five more minutes and his day would begin. Hours filled with Toni easing his emptiness over losing Meg, crowding out her memory.

Unsettled, he rolled off the bed and pulled on his jeans, taking care with his leg. T-shirt in hand, he left his bedroom and reached the hall bath.

The door clicked then swung inward, steam drifting out.

Unaware of his presence, Toni looked behind herself at something in the bath. Her skin glowed from her shower and smelled of soap rather than her cologne. Her stretchy blue camisole and plaid boxer shorts clung to her damp flesh.

Zach's heart beat violently. The tee slipped from his hand.

He told himself to pick it up and race downstairs before she saw him.

His legs refused to move.

Moisture dripped from her freshly washed hair and rolled down her temple to her cheek. Her thin satin strap fell over her shoulder.

Ignoring it, she lifted a brush to her hair, turned, and froze. Her gaze slipped down his naked chest, paused at his fly, and settled on his erection. Desire quickly replaced her surprise. Her lips parted. A gentle breath spilled out. She looked at him, her gaze receptive and yearning.

He slipped his hand behind her neck and pushed her into the door.

The wood smacked the doorstop and vibrated, matching the sounds from his sprinting heart.

Toni dropped her brush. It tapped across the linoleum.

Her skin was so ungodly hot, Zach thought he might die. He captured her mouth and drove his tongue inside, filling her as much as he could, his kiss savage, uncivilized, and punishing for making him wait . . . for making him want.

She suckled him deeper, her mouth tasting of peppermint toothpaste and female lust. She ran her palms up his pecs, wreathed her arms over his shoulders, and dug her nails into his back, imprisoning him with one leg wrapped around his.

Roused beyond control, he ground his stiffened cock into her mound and angled his mouth for greater penetration.

They made sloppy, lewd, joyous sounds, telling each other and the world they were alive, they deserved this, kissing brazenly for what might have been minutes. When the initial fury ebbed, their passion turned tender and exploring, stoking his desire even more.

Toni melted into him, her chest pumping with her strangled breaths.

Obsessive need sliced through him. He tore his mouth free, heaved air, and stepped back, forcing her leg from around his.

Wearing a disapproving look, she glanced at the space separating them then him pulling her arms from his shoulders.

She slumped. "What are you doing?"

"Shh." He imprisoned her wrists in one hand, lifted her arms above her head, and held them to the door. The wood shimmied again. On a rough breath, he pushed her camisole up, exposing her right breast.

A faint sound rose from her throat, sounding like pure pleasure.

His legs went rubbery. Dizziness hit so hard he had to lower his head to stop it. Her nipple was a paler pink than he would have guessed, tight and puckered, waiting for his mouth.

He made his first lick unhurried, his tongue skimming the hard bud. His next was hungered, his laps exploring the bumpy areola and the creamy skin beyond it.

Air whooshed from her. She sagged against the door.

He tightened his hold on her wrists and cupped her breast, loving its weight and warmth, then drew her nipple into his mouth, sucked hard, soft, then hard again, incapable of settling on either. He wanted to fuck her raw on the bathroom floor, take her to the guest bedroom, tie her to the bed, and do things with her he'd done with no other woman.

Finished with her nipple, he slanted his mouth over hers, accepting her tongue and pulling it deep. He slid his hand over her boxer shorts and cradled her mound. *God, God, God.* His ears rang from too much desire. Perspiration broke out on his chest.

Toni moaned indecently, encouraging him to do more.

He dipped beneath the thin cotton fabric and touched her damp curls.

She spread her legs.

Good girl. As far as he was concerned, they could spend the entire day here.

His alarm shrieked.

She flinched.

He did, too. The piercing wail assaulted the quiet, demanding his attention.

He pulled his mouth free and panted, but didn't budge from the spot, not wanting to leave.

Her breath warmed his shoulder.

He was still trapping her wrists, yet couldn't recall when he'd first done so or when he'd pushed her against the door. Gulping air, he forced himself to release her.

Toni's arms fell to her sides. Her camisole hung limply over her naked breast. With what seemed great effort, she opened her lids, her eyes unfocused.

He couldn't think of anything to say, nor could he leave and quiet the alarm.

She touched him, her face saying she desired more.

His breath hitched. He wanted to suck her fingers into his mouth, needing them on his balls and cock.

Wasn't going to happen. Last night, she'd said she'd return to the circuit in a month from now.

Leaving here. Never coming back.

What then? He didn't know and couldn't promise he'd still desire her or would even miss her. Her time here might prove to be nothing more than a pleasant memory of how he'd allowed himself a few moments of joy.

He tensed from longing so painful he could scarcely breathe. His battered heart resisted, shaking him back to good sense, warning him what he'd been about to do with her.

No fucking way. He pulled her into the hall, entered the bath, and closed the door, locking it.

Toni gripped the stove and steeled herself for the inevitable . . . Zach finally coming downstairs to the kitchen. She'd
been in here for fifteen minutes, dressed to go to the shop,
ready to make him breakfast. If either her job or food were
still on the menu.

Nauseated, she refused to regret his kiss. She burned for
him, wanting his weight and warmth back on her, and inside.

A pulse beat deep within her pussy. It creamed at her
memory of his strong body, sculpted pecs, and masculine
scent.

Stuff she wasn't going to get. She worried what might be
going through his mind right now. How to get her out of his
house and shop?

She dragged in a breath and ordered herself to calm down.
Worrying wasn't going to make things better, though this
endless wait might kill her.

He'd stopped showering minutes ago. His footfalls had
sounded in the hall, the uneven steps telling her his leg must
be hurting again. When he'd reached his bedroom, he finally
shut off the alarm, cutting it off in mid-screech.

Since then, he'd been in his bedroom, slowly pacing from
one end to the other. As he perfected his I'm-firing-you
speech?

Chewing her lower lip, she pushed away from the stove
and crossed to the coffeemaker, anxious to do something —
anything — rather than remain frozen like a helpless victim. If
he smelled breakfast cooking, he might pretend their kiss and
lust hadn't happened. Maybe he'd behave as he had last night
after she'd wiped the sour cream from his mouth.

With the coffee dripping, she draped bacon strips across
the skillet and turned on the burner.

His footfalls sounded in the upstairs hall then the stairs.

Desire mixed with queasiness steamrolled over her.

His footfalls drew nearer. His pace slowed. When his boots

stopped tapping the floor, she looked over.

He stood framed in the doorway, his powerful body straining against his tee and jeans, utterly masculine, sensuous beyond belief. He'd finger-combed his damp hair. His face was freshly shaved, his eyes veiled.

She yearned and worried.

The bacon popped.

He glanced at the skillet and egg carton on the counter then took in her naked feet, blue-jean cut-offs, and aqua tee.

Her nipples constricted with his scrutiny.

He took in a shallow breath and spoke on a ragged sigh. "That shouldn't have happened."

Expecting him to say as much, she faced him. "Why not?"

He lifted his eyebrows. "Why not?"

"Exactly." She turned off the bacon so they could talk uninterrupted. "I enjoyed what happened upstairs and you did, too. We're both adults. We both know what we want. We've known it from the moment I stepped into your garage."

His gaze shifted to the side, then returned to her.

For once, she wanted to be honest and reveal a small part of her heart. "We have a month. Why not have some fun? Why not enjoy it while it lasts?"

He shook his head.

She refused to back down. Even though he could never love her, she still craved his warmth, strength, and presence . . . whatever he could offer of himself that would allow them to get closer, possibly become friends. "Why?" She stepped toward him. "Do you have a girlfriend, a fiancée, or an ex-wife you still think about?"

He shoved his fingers through his hair. "I told you last night, I'm not divorced."

"You told me you weren't married."

He dropped his hand and heaved in a deep breath. "Or involved. With anyone."

If that were true, she didn't understand his resistance to her and was reluctant to question him on it. All that mattered were his actions upstairs. His passion then hadn't been feigned or hesitant. He'd wanted her as much as she craved him.

They had to settle this the way she wanted. "Are you worried I'll want something more than sex? Do you think I'd hold your garage or this place hostage?" She lifted her hand to keep him from answering. "I told you last night at the shop, I'm not a thief. And I'm certainly not going to call in a team of lawyers to slap you with a sexual harassment suit. I'm the one who just spent a few days in jail, remember? You're the upstanding citizen. They'd believe you over me in a heartbeat."

His face flushed. "Good God, I never thought any of that, all right?"

She advanced another step. "Then you're concerned there's something wrong with me or I'll get pregnant? I'm clean and disease free. I'm no fool. I don't want to die for a little sex. As far as having a child, it won't happen. I'm fully protected. I know what it's like to be alone, without a father to protect and love me, and have since my dad passed. I'd never force a baby on a guy who didn't want it. I'd never do that to any child, especially my own."

His features slackened.

He looked lost, precisely as she'd felt for too many years. "What we do together won't hurt you, Zach."

"Why are you so alone? What happened to—"

"Uh-uh. Don't go there. Please." She forced her emotions away, refusing to cry, to let him know how vulnerable she was. "This isn't about my past. It's about here and now. You and me. Having some fun. Then I take off. No harm done. You go back to your life, and I go back to mine."

He covered his eyes but didn't tell her to shut up or leave. His chest trembled from his harsh breathing. Color stained his face.

Looked like desire to her. Passion radiated from him, charging and thickening the air.

Desperate to be in his arms if only for a little while, she had to go for broke. "I know you want me. You've had a hard-on since we met. A few minutes ago in the hall, you proved it." She gestured to the solid ridge behind his fly. "You're hard now."

He gritted his teeth. "So what if I am?"

"Do something about it." *Please.*

A vein bulged on his temple. His chest expanded with his fitful breaths.

Never had she seen any man struggle so hard to control his desires. The other guys she'd known, especially Joe, had shown no concern over crossing boundaries.

Why Zach was so different, she wasn't certain. Nor did she care.

Excitement sang in her blood. She advanced another step, determined this moment would play out even if she had to goad him. "What's the real problem? Are you afraid you won't be able to satisfy me?"

He stilled, not even finishing his breath.

The only sound was the hush from the air-conditioning.

He lowered his hand

Her heart thumped. He looked like a rutting animal — male and feral.

Danger flared in his eyes. "Sweetheart, you have no idea what I can do to you."

"You're right." She held his gaze. "So why don't you show me?"

His face darkened. "That's enough. This conversation is over."

"We're not finished."

"I said, knock it off."

"Make me."

He crossed the room so quickly her first thought was to step back. She stood her ground.

Looming over her, he looked fucking huge and aroused. "What did you say?"

She squared her shoulders. "Make me."

He hauled her into him, his free hand on her throat, thumb beneath her chin, tilting it. "You have no idea what you're asking."

Imprisoned against him, with her mouth so close to his, she could barely breathe. "Show me."

He kissed her deep and hard, taking exactly what he wanted, precisely what she desired.

Sagged against his hard length, she slipped her arms around his shoulders. He cupped her ass and lifted her. With her legs wrapped around his lean hips and ankles crossed, she held on for the ride of her fucking life.

They each fought to control the kiss.

He triumphed, crushing her mouth with such force her teeth bit into her bottom lip.

Wasn't enough.

She gripped his tee.

He staggered forward.

She'd forgotten about his leg, hoping her weight wasn't making it worse.

They bumped into the table. It skittered on the tile floor. Plates and utensils clattered.

He broke their kiss first and snuggled his face against her throat, his lips sucking it, tongue stroking.

Pain seemed to be the furthest thing from his mind.

The heat and desire he generated was nearly too much to endure. Her lungs burned, but she couldn't suck in enough air. She shoved her fingers through his thick, wavy locks, lowered her face to his neck, and licked him.

He trembled and said something crude beneath his breath then moved his head, trying to get her to stop.

No damn way.

On an oath, he tightened his arm around her waist and leaned forward, using his free arm to push the plates and utensils aside. A knife or fork fell to the floor. Its metal tinged against the tile, followed by whaps and rapid rattling from plastic plates.

Once he'd lowered her to the table, he broke her hold on him. "Lie back." His voice rasped. "Arms above your head."

Her sheath pulsed. She slumped to the table and assumed the position he demanded. Her tank top wiggled from her quick breaths.

He slid his fingers beneath her waistband, deeper than he needed to go, his actions deliberately intimate as he unbuttoned and unzipped the garment.

She trembled, loving this.

Breathing hard, he lowered the denim, each inch showing more skin, then stopped dead at her dark curls.

She hoped to crap nothing was wrong.

He looked up, pleasure in his eyes. "You're not wearing panties."

Around him, never. "Fuck me."

Perspiration dotted his forehead. He seemed ready to burst . . . prepared to love.

Hurriedly, he pulled her shorts off and dropped them on the floor, untamed lust in his eyes.

The room spun crazily. She squeezed her fists to maintain some control even though she couldn't wait for him to free his cock and bury it within her, clear to its root, leaving no space between them.

He sank to his knees.

She propped herself on her elbows. "What are you doing?"

"Nothing unless you lie down. Now."

Slumped back to the table, she had to ask the obvious. "Aren't you getting undressed?"

"No talking either. Put your feet on my shoulders."

Spread wide, she shivered at the chilly air falling on her damp pussy and struggled to pull in a full breath.

Just as she succeeded, he burrowed his fingers into her opening.

She gripped the table edge.

With her trapped and held in his indecent embrace, he tongued her clit.

Feelings she couldn't describe surged through her. She gasped.

Taking no heed, he held her clit carefully between his teeth and tongued her hard nub, his mouth hot, silky, and wet.

The act was wanton but also sacred. At this moment, he wanted nothing except her. Thrilled, she surrendered, giving herself fully.

He worked her hard and well, yet when she neared the precipice, he slowed, allowing pleasure to drift away.

No.

She pushed closer to force him into giving her relief.

He abandoned her clit, licked her puffy folds, and lapped her juices. Working her sheath with his fingers, he pulled them out, drove them back inside, then returned to her nub and licked furiously.

It was too damn much, too freaking fast. She ground her teeth, wanting to hang on to the delicious feelings, unwilling to come this quickly.

And didn't. Couldn't.

He was on the move again, ignoring her nub to suckle her inner thighs, lick her curls, and catch a few between his teeth, which he tugged playfully.

She laughed and whined. "Aren't you ever going back to my clit?"

"Not if you keep talking, I won't."

Liking his hardass ways, she zipped it and endured.

He stroked her furry mound, dipped to her cleft, and concentrated on her nub, thumbing it quick and hard.

Gawd. She dug her heels into his shoulders and curled her toes.

He dove in for more, tonguing her, driving his fingers in and out of her pussy, mimicking what his cock would do.

She burst, her climax shooting her every which way, leaving her panting and limp. Held captive by pleasure, she couldn't manage any control or propriety. Her legs bowed outward, further exhibiting her partial nudity.

Taking full advantage, he nuzzled his face against her thatch and pulled in her scent.

For that alone, she'd always want him. No other guy had honored her as he had.

After three tries, she gathered enough breath to speak and beg for more. "Fuck me, please."

He stopped kissing her upper thigh and eased his fingers from her. His strained breaths warmed her skin. "No."

Her heart fell. If he hadn't believed her about being protected, surely he had condoms. A man his age with his obvious sexual appetite would be a fool to neglect the matter.

Disheartened, she didn't want to ask his reasons, but needed to know the truth. "Why not?"

"I'm saving that for tonight." He licked her sensitive clit. "All night."

CHAPTER SIX

Unsettled, Zach slogged through the morning, opening the shop, handing out work orders, adding up receipts, taking payment, his mind continually unfocused, snagging on what had happened this morning at his house and his subsequent promise to fuck Toni all night.

After he'd told her she had no idea what she was asking for.

He hadn't a clue what he was doing. One minute, he'd been ready to flee the kitchen and the complications she represented. In the next, he was feasting on her and enjoying it as he had nothing before.

He rubbed his aching shoulder, trying to relax the muscles and stave off a tension headache. Since he'd lost Meg, he'd contented himself with lovemaking that was relaxing and enjoyable, not reckless, wanton, or wild.

There wasn't anything dainty about Toni. She held nothing back, except her past. She was direct, earthy, sensuous, alive.

God help him. It was only ten o'clock, countless hours before he could close the shop and fulfill his promise to strip her bare and spread her wide, her pussy wrapped around his cock, her flesh yielding and demanding.

He hung his head, wondering what tomorrow would bring after tonight. Just as quickly, his mind shut down, not wanting to go there and consider the consequences.

Exactly as she wasn't. She was the one who'd said they should have some fun.

Made sense. As she'd pointed out, they were both adults.

They'd enjoy each other for a month without strings or regret. Maybe.

She'd surprised him by asking if he believed she'd want something more than sex.

Didn't sound like she thought much of him, while he wasn't certain what he wanted. Afraid to consider the answer, he tried to flee his feelings, but couldn't.

Dammit, she kept changing his mind about things. Hiring her. Allowing her to stay in a house that should have belonged to Meg. Wanting a measure of happiness and peace he'd once craved and hadn't allowed himself for nearly two years.

Indecision crowded him, making his snug office seem claustrophobic.

Noise from the shop bled into here. Machinery whirred, engines raced. Toni, Angel, and Robbie bantered, shouting their comments above the din and the top ten Country-Western hits blasting from the radio.

Toni's earlier words haunted him that her time here wasn't about the past, at least to her. She wanted the here and now. Them having fun. Her taking off and going back to her life as he returned to his.

His stomach churned. He fled his office and took to the street to walk off his tension and avoid thinking. Agitation would have pushed him clear past the town limits if not for his bum knee and leg. Short of the Last Chance Diner, he had to stop, his injured muscles hurting like a son-of-a-bitch.

A surgeon who'd operated on him had warned he might never be the same.

The fool had no idea.

The diner door opened, its bell chiming. An elderly couple left. Conversation and chilled air poured out with them. The day's heat wrapped around Zach, the breeze so dry his skin stung.

Hissing air through his teeth, he entered the diner to sit down and cool off.

At the counter, Em delivered a customer's order and looked up, her smile halting when she saw him. Instantly, she rounded the counter and hurried over. "Hey, what's up? You look weird."

That wasn't half of what he felt. "Leg's hurting."

She arched her eyebrows at his admission, something he'd never done before, always pretending he didn't experience any pain.

"Let's get you a seat. You can have your choice of booths in the back."

"A table up here's fine."

"A booth's better." She slipped her arm through his and directed him to the same table he'd shared with Toni, where she'd gorged on a chocolate chip waffle topped with a mountain of whipped cream and after it, an omelet.

Unexpected and intense affection swept through Zach at her pleasure in eating breakfast. Such a simple thing she'd lacked, but he'd given her. Unable to stop himself, he smiled.

Em studied him. "How about a cup of coffee and a Danish? Made fresh this morning."

Not hungry at all, he lied with a nod. "Sounds good." He eased into the booth.

Em didn't move. "How's your new mechanic working out?"

Better than he might have imagined in his horniest dreams.

Desire buffeted him, snatching his breath. On its heels, fear of new loss and its resulting sorrow returned, squeezing his heart.

Em wiggled her eyebrows. "That good, huh?"

He scrubbed his face with his hands.

Didn't stop her. "Want to talk about it?" She spoke in a motherly voice even though she was only three years older than him. "At least tell me if you two are going to start da-ting."

He dropped his hands and slumped against the vinyl cush-ion. "She's an employee, Em, and only for a month."

"You're actually going to let her go back to that daredevil stuff?"

He chuckled at her absurd question and how appalled she sounded. "It's not my choice."

"Sure it is. You can hire her permanently."

His heart squeezed again. He shook his head. Even if he were nutty enough to consider such a thing, Toni made it quite clear she'd be returning to the circuit, continuing with her own life, leaving him to his.

After a month of sex. Nothing less. Nothing more.

Em leaned against the table. "I don't know why you're denying yourself."

Zach looked past her at the street, recalling how he and Meg once sat in here, discussing their hopes and dreams.

Too quickly, his wife's remembered voice faded beneath Toni's. Throaty. Arousing. Filled with life. Wanting to enjoy things as long as they lasted.

While Em wanted to know why he'd deny himself.

He tried to reason it out, and something inside him shifted. Calm — or maybe it was fatigue — told him what he already knew. He was fucking tired of being lonely.

Toni's seductive and taunting question returned about them having fun.

He breathed deeply as a new stew of emotions whispered through him.

Angel's off-colored remark about a rude customer had Robbie laughing and snorting.

Toni glanced at Zach's office. He still hadn't returned.

Nearly an hour ago, he'd left, his color high, features strained, no different than when he'd been between her legs this morning, refusing to mount her until this evening.

At the time, she couldn't help but argue. "Why wait?"

On his feet, he'd draped himself over her, their noses touching. "Because I said so."

Another argument rose to her throat. Zach dismissed it with his commanding kiss, exploring her mouth ravenously. He'd then captured her wrists and pushed them to the table, deliberately imprisoning her. Proving without words he'd do whatever he damn well pleased, on his schedule, not hers.

If he'd been any other man, she would have kicked him in the balls. Trusting he wouldn't hurt her, she liked his commanding presence and hardcore ways.

Done with their kiss, he'd helped her from the table and pressed close, his mouth on her neck.

Within seconds, she was a blubbering mess, unable to do anything except follow his lead. With her mouth on his ear, she promised him all the carnal delight she felt. "Tonight, I'll do exactly what you want."

"Tonight?"

Oh, he was bad. "Now?"

He gave her a sexy smile, then refused to hand over her shorts, tucking them beneath his arm instead, watching as she finished making the breakfast she'd started.

Although her partial nudity didn't bother her, it sure as hell had an effect on him. Several times, he stopped her from going to the fridge or back to the stove so he could fondle her ass. He traced the tattoo on her right butt cheek of two stars, dark blue and entwined.

She figured he wanted to ask the history behind the design and so much more, especially her past. Thankfully, he didn't.

He'd kept things purely sexual, hauling her onto his lap, directing her to straddle him, her naked pussy kissing his bulge, his worn jeans soft against her inner thighs. Positioned thusly, she'd fed him breakfast, pausing to lick crumbs from his bottom lip and orange juice from the corner of his mouth.

Too many times they forgot about the food, making out instead.

However, no matter how she yielded and responded or kept begging then insisting he mount her, he refused to go further.

On the drive to the shop, she could barely keep still. "What are you planning to do with me tonight?"

He halted at one of the few red lights in town and looked over, his attention travelling from her jutting nipples to her mound, then down her bare legs, ending finally at her toe ring. "Exactly what I want."

Lust blazed in his eyes.

Tonight was going to be something, unless he'd had too much time to think about it and was on the verge of changing his mind.

Toni flipped through the work orders he gave her this morning. All light, girly stuff, as though he didn't want her to get too tired before he took her to bed. Or he was suddenly worried she couldn't handle the more complicated repairs.

She joined the guys. "Where'd Zach go?"

Robbie's face was reddened from laughter. He glanced at the shop office. So did Angel. As one, they lifted their shoulders.

"Does he usually do this?" Yesterday, he hadn't left. Of course, last night they hadn't had an impending date to screw each other raw. Wanting reassurance, she pressed. "Does he generally take off, I mean?"

Angel shooed a fly away. "He probably went to the diner for coffee and one of Em's baked goods. He does that sometimes." He glanced at her clipboard. "You have a question? Something I can help you with?"

Maybe. With no customers or gawkers watching them, she leaned in. "What's wrong with Zach's leg?" She'd wondered if that was why he was hot one minute and pulling away from her the next. Being a guy, he might be concerned his leg would hurt so much it would keep him from performing.

Angel traded a look with Robbie, who appeared equally uncomfortable.

She hadn't expected their reaction. "What?" Before either could answer, her heart caught. "Does he have an artificial limb?"

Robbie made a face. "Oh hell, no."

Angel cleared his throat and spoke in an even softer voice than usual, just loud enough for her to hear him over the radio. "He almost lost his leg, but the doctors operated like a dozen times and were able to save it."

"Oh my God, what happened?"

The young men exchanged another glance. Robbie ran his palm over his spiky hair and shrugged. "He was in an accident."

Angel nodded. "About two years ago. With his wife."

Toni's belly knotted. Heat surged to her cheeks, stinging her skin. This morning, she'd worried he had a girlfriend, fiancée, or ex-wife he still wanted. He'd assured her he wasn't involved with anyone.

She didn't want to know but had to ask. "His wife didn't make it?"

"The paramedics did everything they could." Angel shrugged. "But it was real bad."

Robbie stuffed his hands in his pockets. "They'd just bought this big house outside town. They were going to turn it into a bed-and-breakfast for Meg to run. Meg was Zach's wife. They were fixing it up, moving stuff from their old house to there."

Angel cut in. "From what we've heard, Meg was tired, but

Zach wanted to do one last run with their things. It wasn't late. Barely seven o'clock. They were in his pickup when a car ran a red light."

"The kid driving it was a tourist." Robbie made a derisive noise. "He was texting. Never even saw them. He broadsided Zach's pickup at fifty miles an hour, hitting Meg's side. You think it would have killed the fucker, or at least hurt him, but the piece of dirt walked away without a scratch. In fact, he ran from the scene. Cops had to go to his mommy and daddy's vacation house to arrest him."

Angel looked from Robbie to her. "Zach's always blamed himself, even though it wasn't his fault. I mean, how can you know something like that's gonna happen?"

"Probably why he hasn't dated much since Meg died." Robbie glanced at Angel, then spoke to Toni. "For the last year, Em's tried to fix him up with every single woman in town and beyond, but for the most part he's not interested."

Shaking his head, Angel walked backwards to the Honda Civic he'd been working on. "He's a guy, and he'll have his fun, I'm sure, but he's never going to want any woman like he wanted Meg."

Shortly after one o'clock, Zach returned and settled in his office. Toni wasn't certain what she expected, but a glance her way or a simple 'hi' would have reassured her everything was all right between them.

She tried to catch his mood, but his back was to the window.

Her pulse raced, desire for him warring with disquiet at what the guys had told her. For the last few hours, with her mind focused on his love for Meg, she kept making stupid mistakes on the repairs, misdiagnosing some problems, missing others.

Gently, Angel and Robbie had corrected her, pretending

her blunders were no big deal.

Even if they weren't, what had happened to Zach shouldn't have affected her so deeply. Sure, she empathized about his loss. She'd experienced crushing heartache when her dad had died and still felt pain at times. But the truth about Zach's past also confirmed what she'd already known and had tried to forget. Her foolish notions of having a man like him protecting and cherishing her were only a fantasy. He was a young, healthy guy who needed sex, not love, especially from a woman like her.

To him, she'd always be a stranger whose past he'd never know. In a month, she'd leave. There wouldn't be any regrets on his part, nor could she allow any on hers. She'd have a purely physical relationship with him, allowing herself some kind of connection, no matter how meager or fleeting.

When she took off, she'd treasure the memories they'd made, hoping they'd ease the loneliness she'd known for too many years.

"Toni."

Her breath caught at his voice.

He stood in the door to his office. "Stop whatever you're doing and come in here."

She couldn't move, afraid to know why he wanted to see her. His reasons couldn't be good. He wasn't smiling and he certainly didn't look turned on, but all business, like a boss who has an unpleasant job to do, like firing an employee.

He lowered the blinds over the window and closed them.

Oh, shit. This was it, her last moments in this place. He'd had time to think about tonight and had changed his mind concerning their plans. No surprise he wouldn't want her around after that. She'd practically forced herself on him at breakfast, reading more into his momentary lust than she should have.

Tears burned her eyes. Sorrow threatened to overwhelm,

but she shoved it away. When he ordered her to leave, she'd do so with dignity, taking what little money she'd made. She'd ask for work at every other place in Indulgence, and if no one hired her, she'd move on to the next town and the next, doing what she needed to survive.

What she'd grown used to and expected since she was fifteen.

She trudged past Robbie and Angel. Engaged in their work, they didn't bother to look up, unaware anything was wrong.

It wasn't. She'd get through this and whatever else came her way.

She reached the jamb.

Zach looked up, whatever went on inside him hidden from her. "Close the door."

Her stomach knotted. He didn't want an audience to whatever he intended to say. Without comment, and certainly without a futile plea to let their arrangement stand, she eased the door closed, making certain her movements were gentle, not harsh.

"Lock it."

She wanted to be sick but did as he'd ordered and faced him, braced for the worst.

He moved into her so fast, she stepped back instinctively. Her hip hit a cabinet and the metal rattled.

With one arm around her waist, he pulled her into his solid length, cupped her head, and swooped down, imprisoning her mouth with his.

Surprise stole her breath. Yearning took over, defeating what little defense she'd built against him. She sagged against his bulk, her knees bumping his, and held on for dear life, wanting him as she had no other man.

His tongue filled her so well, his firm embrace was so welcomed, the room spun. She made sounds she'd never heard before.

He abandoned her mouth and pressed his lips to her ear. "Quiet. Do you want the guys to hear?"

Breathless with arousal, she could barely manage words. "I don't fucking care."

Subdued laughter vibrated his chest.

She tried to quiet him with her kiss, but he wasn't having it. He stepped back and turned her to face the cabinet and the front door to the shop.

He'd closed those blinds, too. Scant space remained between them and the door frame for someone to peer inside . . . unless they came in.

She kept her voice low. "Did you lock the front door?"

"Not till closing. I've a business to run."

She almost laughed at his ludicrous comment, but couldn't. He unzipped her overalls.

Holy hell.

He sneaked his hand inside the garment, rushed straight past her tank top and bra, and claimed her nipple.

She slumped against the cabinet, jiggling the metal. His touch warmed her more than the Arizona sun. His calloused palm felt better than a clean, safe bed to stay in at night. She bit her lip to keep from crying out in pleasure.

He sucked her neck.

Exquisite feelings curled within her pussy and trickled to her thighs.

She couldn't imagine where he'd been these last hours or what had caused such a change in him from when he'd left. Not that she'd ever question it. This was wicked good.

He pulled her closer and ground his erection into her ass.

She blew out a breath.

"Quiet." He cradled her face, eased it to him, and captured her mouth.

His kiss was greedy, without finesse, his lust telling her he couldn't help himself. Her spirits rejoiced, while the truth nagged. He'd loved Meg, a depth of emotion he'd never give her.

Ignoring sorrow, she told herself it was okay. At least he wanted her. A few minutes ago, this was more than she'd hoped for. Eyes closed, she allowed him what he willed and she desired. Hunger for him pulsed through her, forcing air from her lungs, dampening her channel.

He squeezed her breast firmly, not painfully, finished his kiss and pressed his lips to her ear. "Someone's coming to the door."

She hoped he was kidding.

He turned her around quickly, zipped her overalls, and swatted her butt. "Back to work."

She couldn't budge. Her legs were too shaky, breathing past hard.

Sin flared in his hooded eyes. "You want more?"

Hell yeah. A lot. He'd awakened her desire not only to be pleasured, but taken and dominated, something she'd allowed no man. He was different. He'd play those wanton games for fun and pleasure. "Later. Whatever punishment you decide."

Surprise touched his features. "You mean like spanking?" He looked amazed. "You like to be spanked?"

Only if he was the one doing it. She stroked his fly. "I like a strong man who takes charge and teaches me how to obey in bed." Words she'd never said before, but ones that aroused her now.

"You're sure?"

Rough desire sounded in his voice. She matched it with her own. "Very."

"I'm going to hold you to that." He smacked her ass again.

Her cheeks burned and her heart sang.

As she opened the door leading into the bays, an elderly female came in through the front entrance.

CHAPTER SEVEN

For the first time in nearly two years, Zach didn't dread going home. Toni's desire for him, the way she felt in his arms and how she tasted pushed away his grief and remorse. The magic she'd done on him might not last, but he sure as hell wasn't going to deny himself tonight or in the coming days.

Never had he behaved with any woman in his office as he had with her. Somehow, stealing a frantic kiss and indulging in foreplay seemed reasonable. No—fucking needed.

And talk about his surprise that she liked being spanked. Who would've guessed?

He should have. Uninhibited games were pure Toni and he was ready to do everything she wanted—both shameless and tender—with no regret because this was about sex, nothing more. She'd said as much. No reason for him to feel bad or trouble over their limited connection. He'd have her all to himself, naked and willing, her comfort meant for him alone during the next four weeks.

If she ever got a move on tonight. *What are you doing?* She'd been in the garage bathroom for what seemed an eternity. A half-hour earlier, Angel and Robbie had asked her to have a beer with them. She'd turned them down gently, saying she had other plans.

Fucking A. Now, it was only her and him.

He jiggled his keys, frustrated at the time she'd already wasted, maybe primping when it wasn't necessary. He liked her as she was: natural, free-spirited, pure female. Never had he been so eager to get on the road, go home, do whatever they willed, then stay wrapped within her arms, his cock nestled inside her pussy, protected by their sexual cocoon until daylight forced them back here.

He hauled in an uneven breath.

The door opened. She turned off the light and fan, her face washed, hair combed, dressed in her street clothes.

God, you're beautiful.

Rather than face him as she'd done in the past, she snuck a peek, oddly shy as though she was already playing their games or didn't know what to expect.

She hadn't a clue. Throughout the endless hours, he'd planned every moment for their night, including her willing submission to his dominance that he wanted to explore. But only with her. She'd stirred something deep within him, bringing it to life.

With measured calm that contradicted his pressing need, he took in her sexy toe ring, edged up her milky calves and thighs to her luscious hips, erect nipples, parted lips, flushed cheeks, and seductive eyes.

Her previous hesitation was no more than a memory. On a sensuous smile, she advanced, her steps fluid, her swaying hips oh-so female. When they were only a breath away, she halted, tilted her face to his, and trailed her fingers from his tee to his fly.

Pleasure raged through him. He had to fight from taking her in one of the cars. That wouldn't do. No matter the games they played or the personas they took on, he needed tonight to be special for them. Pure wonder.

"Careful." She spoke no louder than a murmur. "Keep looking at me like that and you may burn out your retinas."

His shaft hardened painfully at her smoky voice, effortless sensuality, and the cockiness he so enjoyed.

She stroked the bulge between his legs, paused on his balls, and traced their contours.

Astonishing delight shot up his torso and down his thighs,

generating feelings he didn't know he had. Again, he struggled against his reckless lust and fantasy of bending her over the hood on the nearest vehicle, lowering her cut-offs, and taking her from behind while the town went about its business just outside the closed metal doors.

You're goddamn crazy. It felt good. He pulled himself together and panted his words. "You kept me waiting too fucking long." He took her saddlebag, settled his free hand on her neck, and drew her into him.

Her blush deepened. Expectation and joy glittered in her eyes.

Liking her reaction, he brushed his lips over hers, his touch light and teasing, her mouth's sweet silkiness and warmth registering clear to his scalp. "Don't do that again."

Without kissing her, he lifted his head and straightened.

She made a face. "Fine. From now on I'll rush. But why'd you stop? Don't. If you want me, take me in your office. We've already broken it in."

"No. Tonight, I call the shots."

She gave him a look.

He stroked the swell of her breasts.

Her eyelids slid down. She leaned into him. "You run things during the day, too."

"Yep, and that's not going to change. Come on."

On the drive to his house, he didn't police his movements. With one hand on the steering wheel, he used the other to explore her inner thigh. Just yesterday, he would have considered his behavior reckless, considering the accident and its aftermath. Since then, he'd always kept both hands firmly on the wheel, his attention ever-vigilant for the unexpected.

He certainly hadn't predicted Toni arriving at his garage yesterday or being with him again tonight, partially tamed to his desires. With her at his side, he experienced more than passion. He felt strangely invincible, as though nothing bad could happen to either of them.

He slipped his fingers beneath her shorts.

She slumped in her seat and opened her legs, allowing him what he willed.

There weren't enough days to satisfy his escalating desire. He touched her damp, fragrant curls.

She made a pleased sound.

A stop sign loomed close. With no one on the road in any direction, he eased far onto the shoulder, safely away from possible traffic, and put his pickup into park.

She craned her neck, taking in their location, then gave him a questioning look.

He tugged her tank top and bra strap over her shoulder, not stopping until he'd exposed her breast.

Surprise and approval shone in her eyes.

Baby, you haven't seen anything yet. He spoke with authority. "Keep an eye out for traffic."

"Are you kidding?"

"Just do it." He drew her nipple into his mouth and sucked as hard as he dared, exactly as he had this morning, learning what she liked.

She moaned softly and clutched his head to keep him at his task.

There wasn't another place on God's good earth he'd rather be.

He breathed in as much as he could, taking in the cologne she'd sprayed on her throat in the bathroom. Beneath the sweet fragrance, her musk drew him like a starving man to food, guiding his free hand to her pussy.

She spread her legs wider.

Her willingness touched him in ways he hadn't thought possible. She was a gift he couldn't resist and needed more than he'd imagined.

For his remaining days, he'd always remember this

moment: her eager surrender and his decision to enjoy her here.

Unobstructed wind buffeted his pickup, shaking it as he would their bed when he thrust into her repeatedly, sating her and himself. Sand and gravel flew against the vehicle, sounding like sleet during a raging storm, its fury matching his pounding pulse.

Latched onto her nipple, he indulged in her fragrant and supple flesh, undid her shorts, and snaked his fingers clear past her mound to her damp, slippery cleft.

She choked out a moan.

That was more noise than he could make, her wet heat mesmerizing him.

With her heels dug into the cab floor, she lifted her ass, giving him greater access.

He rubbed her rigid clit.

"Yes! God, *yes*." She gripped his skull harder and rocked into his touch, telling him she wanted more and demanded completion.

Determined to deny release for the moment, to prove he commanded and she obeyed, he slowed his strokes then stopped.

Her mouth hung opened on her heaving breaths. She pounded the seat. "What are you doing?"

"Driving." With his vehicle in gear, he glanced in every direction. They were still the only ones around. He pulled back onto the asphalt.

Toni sagged against her door and stared at him.

Her scrutiny and pent-up desire pleased him beyond reason.

She cleared her throat. "I know I keep asking the same thing, but I gotta know. Why'd you stop this time? Why didn't you let me come?"

He smiled.

"Oh, come on. That's no answer." She leaned toward him, her hand on his rigid cock. "What are you planning to do with me tonight?"

Whatever the fuck he wanted, exactly what they both required. He eased her hand from him before he got too excited and caved to her demands. "Sit back and behave yourself."

"Sure you want that?"

He stifled laughter and drove as quickly as safety allowed.

She tapped her foot. "We are going to make love, right? You and me, together? No interruptions, no making either of us wait? That is the plan, correct?"

He patted her thigh, refusing to answer her questions about this evening or the few others they'd share.

Only a month.

Yesterday morning, when she'd arrived tired and thirsty, nearly out of luck and hope, thirty days would have seemed like an eternity to him. Because he hadn't known her or started to like the person she was.

Tonight though . . .

One full day had nearly ended, their time together seeming to whiz by far too quickly.

Absorbed in thought and endless desire, he didn't remember the drive home.

He gestured her into his house and dropped her saddlebag in the foyer.

Toni's pulse jumped at the solid thud and the fact they were finally here. *Showtime.* Now what? If things had been up to her, she would have jumped him where they stood and left the other rooms for later, determined they make love in each.

Uncertain whether he'd like that, she waited for him to approach her first, hoping he wouldn't make her wait too long. She only had so much self-control.

Wearing a roguish grin, he inclined his head toward the stairs.

She led the way, acutely aware of him following, his boots slapping the hardwood floor, the sounds far slower than the blood pounding in her ears. She took the first step.

Zach grabbed her wrist, his hold firm and uncompromising. A man who knew what he wanted and wouldn't be denied.

Her heart snagged on a beat. In the few seconds they'd been inside, his demeanor had grown more intensely male, almost wild.

Excitement constricted her throat even as she softened with female need. She wanted his imprisoning weight on her, his passion uncivilized and reckless.

The same as hers.

Yet she held back, conscious of how she looked after a day at the shop, no matter how thoroughly she'd cleaned up. For him, she wanted to be freshly bathed and perfumed, completely feminine, fragile, helpless against his masculine strength. The kind of woman he surely preferred. Not one who could talk and repair engines and hold her own with most guys.

She cradled his face with her free hand. "Let me take a shower before we do anything."

He tightened his grip, confining her further though nowhere close to causing discomfort. "No."

Surprised, she still had to reason. Lust was one thing. Romance another. "It'll only take a few minutes." She sweetened her argument. "We can shower together."

He glanced at her pussy. "I want you naked. Now. Take off your clothes. Don't make me wait."

She snuggled against him. "And if I do?"

Unbridled need darkened his complexion. Frustration hardened his features. "Strip. Now. The shoes and shorts first.

Or I'll have to punish you."

Ah, he wants to play. She should have guessed and had no objections. They could still bathe before they made love, which they would. Heat surged to her throat and cheeks, along with anticipation she'd rarely known.

Longing to draw out their sexual game, to stoke expectation until she couldn't bear it any longer, she stepped down and kicked off her flip flops. The rubber tapped the floor. She pulled her shorts off faster than she ever had. The crotch was damp from her earlier arousal in the pickup.

She dropped the garment and faced him, legs parted, arms to her sides, flaunting her partial nudity, showing him the power she possessed.

He hauled in a meager breath and put out his hand. "Give me your cut-offs."

She delivered them.

He pressed his face to the crotch, inhaled deeply, and made a tortured, wanting noise.

His impassioned response cracked open the walls she'd built around her heart. Him liking her scent and enjoying her as a woman was the greatest compliment she could have received. She was enough for him, no longer a homeless stranger but a worthy partner for their shameless play. A dull ache settled in her pussy, demanding attention, begging for relief only his fingers, mouth, and cock could provide.

He didn't give it. Determination flashed in his eyes, his shoulders tensed, desire restrained.

Her shorts slipped from his hand. He regarded the dark curls between her legs.

She grew wetter, her sheath prepared for his ruthless penetration, his beefy cock buried deep within, his balls smacking her ass.

He crowded her. "Lose the top and bra."

Moments earlier, a bath had seemed the most practical

thing to do. Now, she hungered to bring them to a new level: wanton, primitive, unrestricted. She smiled. "Make me."

In one fluid movement, he propped his foot on the bottom stair and pulled her over his good leg, exposing her naked ass.

Damn. She gripped his thigh. "Go on, do your worst, you'll never get me to obey."

He stroked her buttocks and explored the furrow between her butt cheeks.

A pleasant shiver ran through her. She lost all coherent thought, the feelings he created amazing and sorely desired. Behaving as seductively as a cat, she rubbed against him as much as she could.

He clamped her waist, restricting her further, her flesh exposed and vulnerable to him.

Air spilled from her. She forced down a swallow.

He touched her cleft.

Greedy for what would come next, she lifted her buttocks and delivered herself to him.

A rough sound mingled with his hard breathing. "Yeah, that's it. Show me how much you want this." He ran his fingers down her damp seam and circled her nub, careful not to stroke it.

Forgetting their game, she lost control. "What are you doing? Touch my clit, dammit. Give me some fucking peace!"

"Not until I say so."

Fuck. She dug her nails into his thigh.

Didn't faze him. He played with her plump folds and juicy opening so ready for his cock, but made certain not to come too close to her most sensitive area. The few times he relented and did touch her there, the contact proved maddeningly brief.

You're killing me. Desperate for relief, she had to prod him into action. "What's the matter? Did you forget what to do next? If you want, I'll be happy to remind you how to pleasure a woman."

His fingers stalled near her clit. Seconds passed, the silence growing ominous.

She couldn't have pushed him too far. Reluctant to take a breath, she waited for his next move and her possible apology, explaining how she was only playing.

He stroked her ass gently.

Preparing it for what would soon come? A punishment she needed and desired?

Yes, please.

He traced her tattoo.

New expectation built, driving her wild. Chilled air poured from the ceiling vent, intensifying her vulnerability and partial nudity. She wiggled.

He pressed against her waist. "Stop squirming."

"Or what?"

"What do you think?"

"I don't know. Show. Me."

He smacked her ass, the crack surprisingly loud. A sharp sting followed.

Her breath whooshed out and her sheath pulsed.

He touched her cheek. "Was that okay? Are you all right?"

Better than she'd been in years. "Why'd you stop?" She growled. "You keep doing that. Don't. I mean it."

He leaned down. "You haven't had enough? You're still not going to obey?"

Not even close. "No."

He swatted her again.

"Do. Not. Stop." She begged as she never had. "*More.*"

He complied, exactly as she wanted and had fantasized about, virile and commanding. Quick heat radiated from her spanked cheeks. Her pussy couldn't have gotten wetter.

Panting, he pulled her up and into him, capturing her mouth.

She accepted his tongue and sucked it hard as he preferred.

With his hands on her stinging cheeks, he hauled her mound into his shaft, proving his masculine power.

She drooped against him, ready for his cock, desiring everything.

Too quickly, he finished their kiss and gulped air. "I want you naked."

She wanted him to fuck her until she couldn't take anymore.

Unwilling to voice any demands he'd surely deny, she remained chastised—for the moment. On wobbly legs, she stepped away, pulled off her tank top, and tossed the garment at his feet. A carnal offering. Before removing her bra, she pulled out Belle and Lucky's photo.

Zach's lust ebbed to tender regard. He extended his hand.

She placed the picture in his palm, knowing he'd treat it well.

Carefully, he slipped it inside his front pocket, then became authoritative, looking down his nose at her, a wordless command for her to continue.

She needed no direction in this. Since becoming a woman, she waited to meet a guy like him and wanted to give him everything she had. Rather than toying with her bra clasp, she quickly separated the front tabs and allowed the cups to fall to each side, exposing her breasts.

Cool air licked her areolas, tightening them, hardening the tips.

With great gentleness, he eased the straps down her arms. The satin strips whispered over her. At last the bra fell to the floor.

Nude, she welcomed Zach's scrutiny, the color rising in his cheeks, his mounting need for physical intimacy, matching her own.

It took enormous will not to sink to her knees, expose his

cock, and press her face to it, filling herself with his scent prior to taking his full length into her mouth.

He toed her bra away from her feet. "Turn around. I want your ass facing me."

Her heart missed a beat at what he had planned. For once, she was glad he hadn't told her. She was beginning to like his surprises. They didn't hurt. They aroused and pleased.

Momentarily tamed, she did as he wanted, thinking he might order her to all fours and demand she lift her spanked ass so he could mount her from behind. After taking her vaginally, he might enjoy her anally too, determined to use her most intimate opening before they even reached a bed.

He said nothing, nor did he touch her.

She felt his gaze sweeping over her shoulders, back, waist, and finally her butt, reddened and rosy from her punishment.

What was he thinking? Planning?

Anticipation swirled within her, making her restless.

Their labored breathing filled the silence. The rough sounds mingled with wind brushing against the house and a clock ticking loudly from a room. A noise she hadn't noticed before, though that was no surprise. He'd captured her full attention.

Never had she felt as naked or allowed herself such vulnerability with a man. Her chest tightened, not allowing a full breath. Her knees ached from tightening them.

He rested his hand on her shoulder, his work-roughened palm hot and dry against her skin.

She suppressed a delighted shiver.

With his free hand, he stroked her ass, then the ultra-sensitive area around her tightest opening, and her inner thigh.

Her breath rushed out. She sagged into him, her head against his shoulder, her will fully conquered. Whatever he did, she'd welcome it . . . she'd beg him for it.

He pressed his lips to her ear. "Upstairs."

What? No. She didn't want to move away from his heat and strength. A protest rose to her lips.

"Now, Toni."

He'd spoken softly, rather than barked his order, the low volume adding to his power.

She looked over and became lost in his gaze, wanting things from him she shouldn't. More days. Friendship. A relationship. *Don't go there. Enjoy this.* Too easily she switched to her tough-girl act. "Or what?"

He squeezed her ass, the skin still sensitive from his discipline.

No way would she complain. Wanting more of his dominance, needing him inside her, she padded up the stairs and reached the halfway mark before he followed.

The distance between them must have given him a good view of her cheeks bouncing with each step and her furrow separating, perhaps showing him her anus.

She prayed that excited him.

She had no illusions about being beautiful, nor could she allow herself to hope this would turn into anything more than sex.

He found her attractive. He was lonely.

So was she.

For a brief time they'd ease each other's pain and then move on to wherever life took them, to whomever they met at the end of that road.

She imagined what her heart wouldn't allow: Zach waiting for her in the bedroom, kitchen, pool, giving her his smile, opening his arms, offering comfort, peace, a future and home.

No. She pushed her crazy thoughts away, refusing to indulge in a fantasy that had no hope of coming true.

They were going to have serious fun. Hopefully, he'd remember some of it.

For her, these days would always be in her soul and heart,

the memories soothing those future nights when she was by herself on the road.

Despair pressed close as it always did. She shoved it back down where it couldn't bother her.

Upon reaching the landing, she stopped, again waiting for his direction.

He paused on a step well below her, his mood changed, passion gone, something else replacing it. Doubt?

Oh hell. He couldn't stop now. He owed her thirty days. He'd promised. She didn't want to be alone so soon. She needed at least a week, maybe more, to harden herself to her future. Once he ended things, she'd die a little more inside.

A practical person would have asked what difference it made getting dumped later or now? To her, it was a too swift end to something wonderful she hadn't believed existed. However, her sappy hopes didn't change reality. She had no choice except to face whatever he was thinking. "What's wrong?"

He raced up the steps two at a time, his leg forgotten for the moment, and eased into her, claiming her mouth, kissing her deeply, touching her breasts, buttocks, and pussy, then taking the same journey again. Telling her he didn't know where to linger. Warning her he knew what she did . . . they had so little time.

He kissed her frantically, his actions saying he needed to take as much as he could while afforded the opportunity.

She responded as fully as possible, molding herself to him, burrowing her fingers in his silky hair.

His frenzy paused, but he didn't break away as she'd feared. His kiss turned exceedingly tender and exploring, his lips caressing hers, making this intimacy more potent than his previous ardor.

Tears threatened. She squeezed her lids, denying any sorrow or foolish optimism, welcoming nothing except raw physical pleasure.

She cupped his sac and cock, running her thumb over the succulent package.

His kiss transformed from tender to demanding, then relentless, a shade below brutal.

She didn't mind, loving everything he did.

He tore his mouth from hers.

Okay, she wasn't crazy about the way he kept stopping. Afraid to ask him what was wrong this time, she kept her peace, grateful for the moment.

With their cheeks pressed together, he trailed his hands over her.

She snuggled into his embrace, content to remain like this for as long as he desired.

He allowed them no more than a few seconds before he wrapped his arm around her waist and led her down the hall.

They passed her bedroom. She hadn't expected that. "Where are we going?"

He stopped outside the hall bath. "Here." His eyes sparkled with pleasure. "I'm going to wash every part of you and then I'm going to take you in whatever fucking way I please."

CHAPTER EIGHT

Steam rose from water spilling into the clawfoot tub. Zach added lavender-scented bath oil that hadn't been in here when Toni showered this morning. She suspected his absence from the garage took him to a bath and body shop so he could buy the fragrance she always wore and loved.

Her heart opened a little more at his thoughtfulness, a romantic gesture she'd received from no other man. One she'd always cherish.

She stroked his shoulder. "When are you going to undress?"

He tested the water temperature then shook his hand, flinging away the moisture. "When I'm ready."

She wondered if the scars on his leg troubled him. If he worried she'd find him inadequate because he wasn't perfect.

As far as she was concerned, no man alive could come close to how awesome he was. Looks didn't matter to her, a guy's heart did, along with him being fair, having a great sense of humor, laughing easily, being slow to anger, not holding a grudge.

Zach had those qualities in spades and he was also hot.

For years life had dumped on her, delivering one brutal blow after the other. How she'd managed to get so lucky with him, she didn't know but thanked whatever spirit or god had sent her to Indulgence.

She rested her palms on his pecs, loving how they jumped beneath her touch and his fierce heartbeat. In that, they were alike. If her excitement kept mounting, she'd pass out from too much stimulation. "I want to strip you." Not waiting for his agreement, she tugged his tee from his jeans and lifted the soft cotton past his torso and above his chest.

He was nothing except firm flesh, golden from the unrelenting Arizona sun.

Enthralled, it was all she could do to keep from moaning. Controlling herself, she licked his ruddy nipple.

A lusty and pleasured groan tore from him.

Encouraged, she laved his nipple with her tongue, noting its tiny bumps and his skin's faint saltiness. She trembled, eager to get this show on the road. "Lift your arms."

He kept them at his sides. "I thought I was running this show."

"You are." She gave him a servile look. "I just want to pull off your shirt. It's hot in here. I'm perspiring. So are you. Actually, worse than me."

He struggled not to smile, but did as she asked.

Stoked, she pulled the tee off, tossed it into the hall, and pressed her face to his chest, loving his utter masculinity and natural scent.

He panted.

She licked each nipple and played with the hair in his pits.

Laughter bubbled from him. "What in the fuck are you doing?"

Being herself. Thankfully, he liked that. "Whatever I want."

"Uh-uh. No fucking way. I call the shots."

She fondled his balls.

He moaned.

Now who's boss? "Let me undress you. I swear it won't hurt." She unbuttoned his jeans.

He grabbed her wrists, stopping her easily.

She hoped he wasn't worried about his leg. "Please, let me take off your clothes. I want you naked so I can worship your cock."

"Don't worry, you will." He released one wrist, pulled her to the toilet, and sat. "You can take my boots off."

They weren't his jeans and underwear, but at least he was moving in the right direction. Tamed and attentive, she sank to her knees. With his good leg between hers, she tugged hard on his boot. The footwear came off more readily than she would have imagined and impressed her with its weight. She tossed it in the hall.

It thunked.

She bit her lip. "Sorry if I hurt your floor."

He stared at her nipples. "Screw the floor."

That's what she wanted to hear. She tossed his other boot, not caring where it landed. Painstakingly, she peeled off his socks and propped his right foot on her thigh. Although his leg weighed a ton, she was a strong woman, used to physical labor. She kissed his long toes, perfect for such a tall man, and licked their length, ignoring his choking laughter.

He wiggled. "Stop!"

No way. She needed to honor every part of him, beginning here. She pressed her lips to the tip of each toe, then trailed kisses up his foot to his ankle, sucked it, and stroked his sole.

On a strangled oath, he yanked his foot from her, and lifted his chin to the ceiling. "Fuck, I can't stand it."

Now he knew what she went through when he wouldn't let her come. Feeling mischievous, she had to rub it in. "Baby."

He lowered his face.

Water splashed into the tub. Steam crowded the room. Savage lust transformed his features, propriety and civilization gone, leaving only a male determined to conquer a female. He stood, shut off the water, and looked at her.

She pushed to her feet, unfulfilled desire buzzing through her, along with uncertainty as to his next move.

He pulled her to the counter to face the oval mirror, a dated design matching the house. "Bend over."

Her pussy ached for him. New moisture bathed her soft folds. Not knowing whether he'd punish her again or mount her, she gripped the marble counter, arched her back, and lifted her ass, ready for anything and everything.

He met her gaze in the mirror, its corners fogged from steam. Intensity blazed in his eyes. His pecs and biceps bunched with tension, his deliberate restraint. He stepped behind her, unbuttoned his jeans, and yanked down the fly.

Lust heated her skin. Desire left her lighthearted. Soon, he'd mount her, plunging into her depths, taking possession, fucking her until they both screamed in pleasure.

Now, now, now. Don't make me wait any longer. She stretched her neck to check out his cock and marvel at its beauty.

Zach didn't allow it, remaining behind her, shoving his jeans and underwear to just below his narrow hips. Only enough to remove his rigid cock from its prison.

He clamped her hip and brought his rod to her cleft, bathing the head in her slick moisture. His neck muscles corded, shoulders tightened, and his lids slipped down, leaving narrow slits. "Lift your ass." He squeezed her hip, punctuating his command.

On an expectant breath, she obeyed.

He entered her without pause, his thick cock stretching her channel to its limit, opening her to capacity.

Her mouth hung open.

He drove deep, tunneling without restraint until she'd almost contained his full length.

"Holy motherfuck." He panted. "This is so damn sweet. You like?"

She loved his gruff voice, deepened from arousal. "God, yeah. Do. Not. Stop."

He laughed. "Don't worry. This time, I won't." With one

final push, he managed to go deeper, the root of his cock hugged and sheltered by her opening.

She gripped the counter in a futile attempt to steady herself against the feelings rocking her: lust, need, longing so deep it became frightening, battering her heart and soul, encouraging her to yield and make the most of the time they had.

She arched her back as much as she could which tilted her buttocks and gave him greater access.

He released a breath, tightened his hold on her, and pumped.

Her head fell forward, too damn heavy to keep up. "Wow."

Snickering, he brushed her clit — once, twice, three times. Incredible delight shot down her thighs and up her torso. Her pussy clenched around his cock, encouraging him to stroke her sheath and bring her to climax. "Fuck me. Do me hard."

He ignored her plea and circled her nub, rather than touching it. He thrust into her lazily, telling her they had all the time in the world.

Bull. They only had now. Who knew what tomorrow would bring? Crap, she didn't want to consider anything bad. Needing him to pick up his pace, she backed into him.

He stopped. "Don't do that again. I call the shots. You obey."

Yeah, yeah, yeah. "Sure thing, but can't you pump even a little faster?"

"In time." He eased his rod out of her, slipped it back inside at a snail's pace, and massaged her nub lightly, using it at his pleasure, driving her nuts.

She lost it and bumped into him again.

"Toni."

"I can't help myself. Do you honestly want me to play dead?"

He rubbed her clit.

She trembled and gasped.

"You're definitely not dead or playing. You said you wanted a firm hand. Have you changed your mind? Want to do missionary style with the lights off while we're still clothed and have our eyes shut?"

He was being ridiculous, but she got his point. She'd agreed to their game. Hell, she'd encouraged him to dominate her. "No. But don't go too far. I can only last so long."

"You're stronger than you think." He caressed her hip. "You're the strongest woman I know."

His compliment stunned her, as did the passion behind his words. She looked at him in the mirror.

He kept his face down, feelings hidden. Silence pressed in, broken only by a steady drip from the faucet and his forceful breaths. His cock grew harder within her.

She squeezed her pussy around him, thinking he'd like that.

His quick smile said he did.

He eased out of her and thrust back inside with such force, she swayed forward. Again, he plunged into her, bringing more pleasure compounded by him finger-fucking her clit. He matched each powerful stroke from his cock with a delicate one on her nub, his pace still controlled and maddening.

Heat pooled between her legs and narrowed her channel around his male flesh. Her orgasm whispered closer, closer . . .

Despite his vigorous thrusts, he kept his slow, steady pace from earlier. How he managed it, she didn't know. She was losing her damn mind, so focused on relieving the building pressure she couldn't even bitch.

Moisture ran from her temple to her cheek. The room was like a sauna. She'd never been as hot.

He wasn't calm, cool, or collected either. Perspiration coated his chest, his muscles were taut, features tight, his gaze focused on his cock invading and plundering her flesh.

She wished she could see what he did: his shaft glistening from her moisture, the thick, distended veins on the hard column, its flesh reddened with desire and friction from their bodies. His lightly furred balls, rounded and firm, close to his groin, barely swinging with each dominant thrust. His fingertips whitened from holding her hips so tightly.

He drew his thumb over her clit, rougher this time and more prolonged.

Delight she needed and required burst through her, sending warmth and pleasure in too many directions for her to follow. Her scalp tingled, limbs weakened, breathing became impossible, all feeling concentrated in her pussy. She neared the peak.

Zach teased her nub with greater speed and force. He pumped quickly and heatedly, smacking against her.

She gasped, the exquisite reprieve crashing through her, sending her to a place she never wanted to leave.

He pumped twice more and then his delighted bellow filled the room.

The best sound ever. Pleased and panting, she folded her arms over the counter and rested her head on them.

Zach draped his torso over hers, his breaths heating her shoulder, his hand returning to her clit. He brushed her sensitive nub.

She shivered.

He stroked faster.

No, no, no. She was still after-glowing from her climax and couldn't take more stimulation. "Stop. It's too much."

"Sure?"

She wasn't and groaned. "I don't know."

"That's why I'm the Dom." As he sucked her shoulder and trapped her with his size and strength, he worked her clit mercilessly, stirring new desire, more intense than what went before.

Her new orgasm hit, leaving her a hot mess, reduced to drooling and babbling.

He patted her butt cheek. "Good?"

"Uh-huh." It was the only word she could form.

He kissed her back, straightened, and pulled out.

His absence registered instantly, leaving her empty and bereft.

Fabric rustled. A zipper rasped.

That was worse. He'd actually pulled up his jeans and fastened them. Why?

She had no chance to ask. With his arm around her waist, he eased her to a standing position.

Slumped against him, she rested her head on his shoulder and pulled in his scent.

He walked her to the tub. There, he kept her close while he reached down and tested the water. After an abbreviated yawn, he trailed his damp fingers from her throat to her breast.

Her nipple tightened.

"Warm enough?"

"Your mouth would be better."

"Mmm." He sucked her nipples, his coming beard scraping her.

She'd never get enough of him. "This is perfect."

"Maybe." He talked around her nipple. "However, it would take days, maybe a week for me to wash you with my tongue."

"I don't mind."

Chuckling, he helped her into the tub.

At the water's balmy caress every bone she had seemed to dissolve. This was past nice to legendary. With as much grace as possible, she sank into the silky cocoon. Head against the tall back lip, hands on the porcelain edge, she sagged beneath the surface. Fragrant water lapped her areolas. She bent her knees and allowed her legs to dip to either side, exposing herself fully to Zach, inviting him to come inside and join her.

Contentment radiated from Toni, relaxing her features, revealing her underlying vulnerability. So different from the ballsy look she'd given Zach as she'd claimed to be the best damn mechanic around. At the time, he'd also caught despair and caution so deep, he sensed others had hurt her frequently and she didn't know what to expect from him.

Her unguarded trust at this moment humbled him as few things had.

He sensed whatever he proposed, she'd welcome his suggestions eagerly, the same as when he'd spanked her. A stunningly erotic game she'd willingly introduced as though she had no qualms about putting her safety in his hands.

She ran her damp fingers down his fly to his bulge.

Even through the denim, her heat and gentle stroking tightened his balls and dried up his spit.

She made a purring sound. "Take your clothes off and join me. There's lots to see and enjoy." She swished her legs in the water.

Torn between laughing in pleasure and smiling, he settled on the latter. "The tub's not big enough for both of us."

She traced his thickening cock.

He'd been out of her for only a few minutes and already he was ready for more, a record he hadn't experienced in years.

"Mmm." She circled his crown. "You are a huge guy."

Like an idiot teen, he grinned.

She left his balls and cock to kiss his fingers instead, her playfulness gone. "Can I ask you something?"

Her quick seriousness worried him. He didn't want to talk about anything bad or painful. "I guess."

"Thanks. You're tired, right?"

He wouldn't pass up a nap if she offered to share one with him, because she was tired. "Are you asking if I need to sleep because I came? Hell no." He wiggled his eyebrows and smiled. "I'm just getting started."

"Good." She glanced at his knees, then quickly averted her gaze, embarrassment on her face. "But don't you at least want to sit down?"

His smile hung on for a second longer before it felt foolish. She'd noticed again how he favored his good leg, possibly curious what had caused it.

He steeled himself for her expected questions.

They didn't come.

Gratitude washed over him. Tonight, he didn't want to think about the past, preferring to let desire blunt his incessant pain. "I'm fine."

Braced against discomfort, he sank to his knees beside the tub. He selected a sponge from the small cabinet to the side and dipped it into the fragrant water. "Drape your arm over your head."

Toni did as he asked, her gaze never leaving his, her actions fluid with no hesitation or unease. As though having a man bathe her was normal in her world. Maybe it had been.

He squeezed the sponge tighter than he'd planned, wondering about the men in her life, surprised at the jealousy pumping through him.

Ignoring his adolescent reaction, he ran the sponge down her arm, pausing at her elbow. A faint scar he hadn't noticed before marred her perfect skin, this area paler than the rest and puckered slightly. "How'd you get this?" He traced the contours, wondering if a man had caused it. Some bum she'd known. Some prick who'd hurt her.

She stretched her legs and sighed. "Overshot a jump during a performance."

"What?" The scar seemed worse now. "You mean you

crashed?"

"Not even close." She rolled the back of her head against the tub. "Cycle came out with just a few dings, though I hit the gravel pretty hard and tore my jacket sleeve. Cost me big bucks to get the leather fixed."

Her indifference to her health and safety surprised him. He searched for other injuries, didn't see any, but wasn't certain if the water masked them. When he'd been inside her, he was too far gone to spot any wounds or marks. Hell, the house could have been on fire and he wouldn't have noticed. "You've been hurt?"

A throaty chuckle bubbled from her.

He withdrew his hand.

"Whoa, wait. I'm not making fun." She lowered her arm and clawed damp hair from her neck. "Yes, I've been hurt, but only when I screw up, which I don't do that often. Can't afford to keep getting my leather pants and jacket fixed, you know?"

He didn't. She worried more about hurting her clothes than injuring herself, possibly dying. "What exactly do you do in your performances?"

"Just the usual stuff." She ticked off the acts, each new one sounding worse to him than the others.

He cut in. "T-bone? Roll-over? Suicide twist?"

She regarded him, her lids heavy with relaxation or enjoyment, possibly both. "There has to be some danger involved or no one would come to the performances."

And she wouldn't make a living. She wouldn't have a place to stay at night or anything to eat. He couldn't imagine what had brought her to this rather than a normal life with a permanent home, friends, a family to worry about her, and to be there if she needed help. She wasn't uneducated. Her diction and world-view—that she'd unknowingly shared with him at dinner last night—were solidly middle-class.

He recalled Em badgering him about letting Toni return to her daredevil ways. "You like that kind of work?"

She closed her eyes.

Not the answer he wanted. He shouldn't have pried, but couldn't help himself. He worried about her when she didn't. He wanted to shake some sense into her, tell her she deserved more than she'd settled for. But how?

She was a proud woman and would take offense. Hell, if she'd said he'd been a fool for grieving as long as he had, he would have told her his life was none of her damn business.

They'd barely gotten to know each other and already their non-relationship was too complicated. He cursed himself for saying anything. "Look, I shouldn't have asked. It's not my place."

"I'm not mad." She spoke softly, without artifice and looked at him. "My job isn't a question of liking it or not. It's what I know."

He wanted to ask why, and who taught her such a crazy career, and who the fuck had brought her into it, but couldn't. He didn't want to embarrass her or bring her pain.

"It's not all bad." She smiled. It didn't reach her eyes. They looked sadder than hell. "I know my world is a mystery to you and other people who have regular jobs, but what I do does take skill. If you can get the better gigs, the pay is great, better than a wage slave gets for a job that might not be there tomorrow after the powers-that-be sign another trade agreement. And what I do isn't that hard. Hell, even Ann-Margret did some of that stuff."

She'd lost him. "Who?"

Toni laughed, not in derision, but a vibrant sound filled with life.

Warmth engulfed him. He wanted to hug and hold her until tomorrow then call in sick at the shop and spend the new day with her.

Her laughter faded to a chuckle. "Ann-Margret's an old Hollywood star, Lucky's favorite." Her smile widened, lighting up her face. "I bet he's watched *Viva Las Vegas* a hundred times. Ann-Margret starred in it with Elvis Presley. You do know him, right?"

He gave her a look. "I wasn't raised on Mars."

"No one said you were." She patted his hand. "There were some outtakes at the end of the film. In between takes, Ann-Margret horsed around on her cycle, standing on the seat while it was tooling down the road."

He couldn't picture that. Hell, he didn't want to. "You mean, the damn thing was moving and she wasn't even driving it?"

"How could she? She was standing on the seat."

"That's what you do?"

"Absolutely." Toni brightened. "Better than her, I might add. But I'd never say that to Lucky. To him, she's a freaking goddess." She smiled gently. "Belle often jokes that the only reason she started dyeing her hair red was because of his obsession with Ann-Margret. It's not true, of course. They're very committed."

"They're motorcycle performance artists too?"

Her mouth trembled, erasing her smile. Vigilance returned — wariness at what else he might ask. She glanced at the water. "Do you want me to finish washing up?"

"No. I'm going to do it."

She took him in. "You've done this before?"

Never. "You're the first."

Pleasure shone in her eyes, their color so amazing, his heart turned over. "Drape your arms over your head."

She did as he wanted. The bliss on her face, the water sparkling on her skin, brought him back to an X-rated film he and his high school buddies had watched one dateless Friday night. The actress who'd starred in it was frequently wet from the hot tub, shower, or pool where she and the plumber went at each other like there was no tomorrow. Smiling at the memory, he ran the dampened sponge over her.

Once he finished washing her arms and smooth pits, he concentrated on her breasts, taking extra time and care with them.

"I'm losing feeling in my fingers." She lowered her arms. "How about you?"

He played with her nipples. "Mine are great."

"I figured. Enjoying yourself?"

More than he had in years. "Lift your leg."

Water sluiced down her firm flesh.

He held her calf and ran the sponge from her inner thigh to her dark bush.

She murmured a particularly salty oath.

His shoulders shook with suppressed laughter. "Bad girl."

"The worst. Punish me."

He separated her soft folds, plump with desire, and touched her clit.

She tried to move closer, sloshing water over the tub.

Chastising her, as she wanted, he eased his hand away and kept it from her reach.

"Uh-uh. No." She frowned. "Come back here."

"Whatever you say." He latched his mouth on her inner thigh, just below her knee, and sucked.

She inhaled sharply then moaned out the air she'd taken.

With her attention on pleasure, he stroked her nub.

A new oath escaped her. She sighed noisily and slid down until the water touched her chin.

He leaned closer. "You're not about to fall asleep on me, are you?"

She kept her eyes closed. "Uh-uh."

"Good." He rubbed her clit.

She stretched. "Don't stop. I could stay like this forever."

He stroked her clit twice more then withdrew his hand. "And miss what I have in store for you in the bedroom?"

With loving care that surprised Toni, Zach washed her, leaving no part untouched. His meticulousness in here proved there wouldn't be an inch of her he'd fail to claim this night.

Scented with lavender, weakened with need, she grew increasingly lightheaded.

He patted her dry, paying particular attention to her breasts and pussy while sucking her neck.

If she'd known taking a bath would be this awesome, she would have begged him to wash her this morning.

Finished, he dropped the thick white towel near the tub.

Her excitement grew at what he had in store for her in the bedroom. "What have you planned?"

Hunger shimmered in his eyes. "Exactly what I want." Indecency quieted his voice. "What you're going to allow."

She eased into him, her nipples brushing his pecs, her mound to his luscious bulge. "Do whatever you want." She pressed her face to his throat.

He squeezed her tattooed cheek. "I fully intend to. In your bedroom. "He swatted her ass. "Go on. Get in there."

The trip seemed endless. She was too wired from anticipation, her limbs heavy and weak. Once in her room, she sniffed, surprised to smell fabric softener. He must have laundered the sheets while he'd been gone from the garage.

She chucked his chin. "You played hooky from work to do laundry?"

He brushed his mouth over her ear. "I own the place. I can do whatever the fuck I want."

He would too. "The sheets smell good."

"They will when they smell like you and me." His fingers stroked her anus.

Overwhelmed at the intense pleasure, she pushed to her toes.

He eased her back down and kissed her shoulder. "On the bed."

Beyond the filmy curtains, waning sun streamed over the hills, bathing the room in frail, golden light, deepening the shadows, glinting dully off the brass headboard. He'd folded the comforter at the baseboard and removed the pillows. In their place lay a single red scarf.

Either a blindfold, a gag, or a binding. It had no other purpose here.

Her heart skipped several beats.

Displayed on the dressing table were numerous candles in varying heights, each a deep violet shade. Near the largest stood a tiny bottle, the liquid inside a shimmering saffron color in the fading light. Curious, she bypassed the bed and Zach's command to see what it was.

She read the label. Her cheeks burned.

He joined her.

Toni leaned against him, her legs threatening to give out. "Bad boy."

He took the bottle of oil, a lubricant to enjoy anal sex, and put it next to the condoms. Tonight, he'd have her in every way.

She couldn't wait, wanting his touch, kisses, and desire.

He squeezed her ass. "On the bed."

Not wanting to pull her gaze from him, she backed into it, her legs bumping the mattress, pulse racing.

He lit the candles. Their bobbing flames provided a romantic and magical touch, turning the bedroom into a place of refuge, comfort, and unrestrained passion for them, no one else . . . no other woman.

For tonight and the few to follow, she had no doubt she belonged here with him.

Delight and appreciation welled up in her, emotions so strong, she couldn't take a breath. Her eyes filled in happiness, not sorrow. For the first time in too long, she wasn't alone.

She would be again, in a few short weeks, though not now. Concentrating on that, she focused on Zach.

With the last candles lit and their lavender fragrance filling the room, he grabbed the oil and several foil packets. Shadows played across his handsome face and naked chest, enhancing his alluring masculinity. He was nothing but hard angles — firm, muscled flesh that could easily subdue and conquer her, using her as he willed and she craved.

He crossed the room and stopped so close their toes nearly touched.

His beautiful eyes fascinated her. As did his stubble, scent, and strength. She cupped his face, loving how his beard-roughened cheeks bit her palms, and lowered his head, then touched her lips to his.

His breath was sweet and hot. Ambrosia to a lonely woman who'd had to wait too long for this.

She kissed him in a way she had no other man, with a need so fierce it alarmed her. Not able to get enough, she angled her head for deeper penetration, sweeping her tongue around his wet, heated mouth.

He allowed her lust for only a moment before jerking free. With a slightly dazed look, he gestured to the mattress. "On the bed now. I'm not telling you again."

Outwardly obedient, but smiling inwardly, she scooted to the center, lay down, and draped the silk scarf over her breasts, hiding them from him.

He narrowed his eyes, but couldn't stop his smile. "Take it off."

"No."

He planted his hands on his hips.

She figured he didn't like her backtalk. Too damn bad. She offered her own demand. "You do it."

Something flickered across his face. She guessed pleasure at her challenge *and* his determination to tame her.

Good luck with that. If she'd been docile, she wouldn't have been here, their play already at an end. For some reason, he liked her spirit.

She enjoyed his kindness and sense of fun.

He snatched the scarf, placed the oil and condoms on the mattress, and stared at the springy curls between her thighs. "Roll over, on your hands and knees, legs spread, ass lifted."

At the promise of him taking her anally, warmth flooded her chest and throat. Not because she was embarrassed or scared. The act was so decadent it stoked her desire as few things could. Bikers she knew had often complained about vanilla sex, wanting the roughest and rawest ride they could get.

Doing so without respect and tenderness for and from their partner was no more than fucking.

She'd always needed something deeper and told herself with the right man, nothing would be off limits.

Wanting Zach nude, desperate to have him inside her, she rolled over and got into position . . . submissive and exposed, ready for his use.

Shadows trailed over the mattress, bobbling slightly with the candle flames. The air-conditioner clicked off. Coolish air whispered around the room, magnifying her nudity and wanton pose.

He made no move to mount her, nor did he speak.

Keeping her tongue, she waited, willing to have him control the act, to observe every part of her no matter how unnerving the delay might be.

Her breathing hitched and her pussy tightened. She imagined his gaze trailing over her ass, the tattoo she'd gotten to prove she'd always belong in Belle and Lucky's lives. That she was like a real daughter to them, not merely a desperate teen they'd taken in and given a home, then taught her their trade.

She expected Zach to stroke the design as he'd done numerous times these last hours.

He did not. He simply observed while she remained defenseless, skin prickling with expectation, picturing him staring at her openings, desirous of each.

He got on the bed, the mattress dipping beneath his weight. The oil rolled into her knee. Candlelight glinted against the shiny condom packets.

Blood pulsed in her ears.

His command cut through the sound, "Lift your hands."

She hadn't expected that order and now knew why he'd bought the scarf. With her elbows supporting her weight, she did as he wanted and laced her fingers.

He looped and knotted the silk around her wrists, then tied the ends to a rod in the headboard, imprisoning her.

Instinctively, she tugged on the binding to test it.

"Yank all you want." His rich voice rumbled with domination and excitement. "You're not getting free." He boldly stroked her anus.

Her breath caught.

"You won't be free for a very long time." Offering her no chance to respond, he knelt between her legs and grabbed the oil. The cap made a small cracking sound—him breaking the seal.

He stroked the warm, satiny fluid on her tight ring and worked his finger past it to lubricate her opening for his hard, fleshy cock.

The act was decidedly intimate and wonderfully base. Desire for it and him pulsed through her, wobbling her arms and legs.

His zipper rasped, fabric swished . . . him shoving down

his jeans and underwear.

His silky hot cock skimmed her thigh.

She grunted, unable to form words, even to demand that he enter her.

He combed her dark curls with his fingers and reached her clit. With his free hand, he lifted his shaft to her pussy and plunged inside.

She started at the intimate assault, not expecting him to take her vaginally. Pleasure followed, wanton and lewd, at his brisk thrusts into her—quick, hard, and tireless—while he also stroked her nub, forcing her to immediate completion.

The climax took her by surprise, happening too soon, sapping her strength.

Within her, his cock remained hard as stone. Not having come, he breathed shallowly.

She suspected to restrain himself.

Determined to prove her power over him as he'd done with her, she worked her sheath, squeezing his cock as hard as she could.

He didn't complain, nor did he spank her. He pulled out.

Crud. She squeezed her fists so hard, her knuckles hurt. She tugged on the scarf, wanting freedom so she could crawl all over him.

Unmoved by her turmoil or simply ignoring it, he returned to her tight ring, his fingers slick from the lube, his stroking slow and sensuous.

The intense feelings he created tempered her movements and scattered her thoughts, reminding her how accessible she was—willingly, wantonly—something she'd done with no other man.

As she fought for each breath and squeezed her lids, his searching, unhurried pace sharpened her senses, sending heated streams to her pussy, constricting those muscles, which delivered additional moisture in response.

Repeatedly and with great deliberateness, he probed her tightest opening, heightening her pleasure in the lascivious act.

She could have done this for hours.

He withdrew his finger.

Hell.

A faint tearing sounded. Had to be the foil packet holding the condom.

He adjusted his weight and the mattress shimmied.

Come on, come on, come on. How long did it take a man to roll on a rubber? Even a second was more than she was willing to wait.

He eased close. His shaft brushed her thigh, its slick warmth startling and arousing.

Her heart banged uncontrollably. She gripped the sheets, prepared for anything, wanting it all.

Gently but with great assurance, he worked his plump crown into her opening, obligating her body to accommodate his.

She had no choice, and wanted none. She'd promised everything, eager to give him still more. He'd touched a part of her denied these last years, the yearning, the hope for something substantial and lasting.

They only had a month.

Reluctant to accept the truth, but grateful for this moment, she gave everything she could and yielded to him. Inch by glorious inch, he burrowed inside, his unsteady breaths matching hers, the pressure from his shaft intense yet welcomed.

On one final push, he sank into her fully, their bodies joined.

She wiggled into him. "More."

Draped over her, his chest slick with perspiration, he touched her clit. "You mean this?" He rubbed.

She bucked into him, driving his cock further inside.

He made a pleased sound. "Too much?"

"Never. Go on." She panted. "Please."

Lips to her shoulder, he tongued her skin and stroked her nub, while easing his shaft from her then plunging back inside.

An act like no other and now theirs alone. A sentimental notion but she couldn't contain her escalating happiness.

For a long time, he rode her, easy and hard, gentle and ruthless, taking his pleasure, delivering striking relief and the priceless hope for more.

CHAPTER NINE

The customer huffed. "So do you?"

Zach looked up from his computer screen at the thirty-something woman who wore her drab blonde hair in a sloppy ponytail. Her sunburned face, pissy scowl, and grating accent marked her as a back-east tourist.

Seconds earlier, he'd stopped listening to her whining and didn't try to pretend otherwise. "Do I what?"

She sighed loudly. "Take American Express." She waved the gold card above her shoulder.

He focused on his computer screen, the research he'd been doing. "Sorry. We only take MasterCard and . . ." His words trailed off as he read the article he'd pulled up.

She huffed out a breath. "How about Visa? Ever hear of it?"

He nodded.

"So do you take it?"

"We do."

"Figures. Here."

The card landed near his hand.

"I'll need my car back by this afternoon. I have to get home. Hell, I can't wait."

"We'll do our best."

She whipped out her smartphone and stomped to the door. While she complained to whomever she'd called about the lousy service and shitty weather in Indulgence, he prepared her estimate, his attention continually drifting back to his computer screen.

She returned to his desk.

He handed her a receipt, along with her Visa and a warning. "If we find something else, it could be more."

"Just fix it. I want to get out of here."

And he didn't? On her snotty departure, he slumped in his chair, looked at the time, and let out a low groan. Only nine-thirty. Practically a lifetime until he could close the shop.

Already four days had passed since he'd first started sleeping with Toni. Instead of their nearly constant sex sating him, he couldn't get enough of it or her. Her throaty laugh, ballsy comments, blue-green eyes, skin too pale for sunny Arizona, her pure and genuine wanting of him stirred emotions he'd locked away for too long.

And the blessed contentment . . .

Eyes closed, he rested his head against the back of his chair and recalled every moment with her, beginning with their first night as lovers.

After he'd taken her repeatedly, he'd slept as he hadn't in years, awakening with her on his mind . . . craving her fragrant, silky flesh against his. Braced for guilt and doubt, along with his usual fear of loss, he'd felt only a pang, surprisingly mild and understandable. His attraction to her simply concerned sex. It wasn't about allowing her into his heart. The pleasure he'd experienced with her was so new and welcomed, little could dilute it.

Even the reality of her leaving in a few weeks.

Staving off the inevitable, he'd reached for her, but found cool sheets rather than heated skin. Not understanding and fearing she'd already taken off, he'd pushed up, heart galloping. No light illuminated the hall from the bath. In the bedroom, the largest candles still burned, eating away shadows, aiding his search.

She touched the glass on the display case filled with dolls, her profile to him, tears sparkling in her eyes.

Startling and deep tenderness rocked him. He recalled

what she'd said her first morning here about knowing what it was like to be alone without a father to protect and love her.

Her sadness told him she was thinking about her child-hood now, the dolls bringing back whatever pain she'd known after she'd lost her dad.

Torn between giving her a hug and intruding on her sor-row, he was afraid to move.

She looked at him, not hiding her sadness.

He left the bed and pulled her close.

She didn't cry, but her weary sighs broke his heart.

If he'd owned the power, he would have given her back whatever she missed and wanted. Impotent against her pain, he stroked her hair and held her gently.

She rubbed her face against his shoulder. "I'm all right."

"I know."

"I had a bad dream."

"It's okay." He didn't want her to have to lie to him. They'd gone beyond such foolishness. She wasn't a stranger any longer, but a woman he genuinely liked, a person he cher-ished. "It's over. Would you like some warm milk to help you get back to sleep?"

"No."

"A beer?" He didn't have hard liquor in the house.

"Uh-uh."

"A snack?"

"I want you."

She sank to her knees and opened the metal button on his jeans, clothing he still hadn't removed.

He cuffed her wrists, stopping her.

"It's okay, Zach." Her voice was husky with emotion. "I know about the accident and how you were hurt . . . who you lost. I'm so sorry."

She'd stunned him to silence, her good heart and sweet concern leaving him helpless against the loneliness he couldn't flee any longer.

With great gentleness, she'd lowered his jeans and briefs, then traced the cruel scars on his leg, some from the accident, others from repeated operations. She'd brushed her lips over jagged skin he hadn't wanted her to see. Cautiously, she'd stroked the uneven surface as though fearing she'd bring him more harm.

He swallowed at the memory. She was so different than the few other women he'd slept with these last years. When he'd undressed with them, they'd quickly glanced away from his hideous scars, repulsed or troubled at what they saw.

Toni embraced his imperfections and him.

His heart twisted with a new emotion, one he wasn't about to identify.

Despite the noise coming from the bays, her voice rose above the din, welcomed, energetic, alive. "Sorry guys, but I have to do laundry and other stuff."

Robbie yelled back, "Ditch it until tomorrow. How can you say no to pizza at Paula's and a few beers?"

Because she'll be with me tonight. And she was still broke.

Zach glanced at his computer screen, the research he'd been doing into her life to find out whatever he could, what she wouldn't tell him, unable to stop himself any longer. From the moment she'd stared at Meg's old dolls, her eyes welled with tears, he had to know where she'd come from, why she'd ended up here, and where she might be going after she left him.

His stomach cramped at the thought.

Ignoring the pain, he concentrated on his search. Tiled on his screen were numerous articles about her and the Starrs. He'd guessed correctly — they'd been motorcycle performance artists. Given the newspaper dates and Toni's youthful appearance in numerous shots, she'd joined their act at sixteen.

A time when other girls were getting involved in cheer-leading, preparing for dances and proms, falling in love with all the wrong guys, worrying their mothers to distraction.

He couldn't imagine where Toni's mom was in this. Why she hadn't stopped what he read about now.

In those early photos, Toni looked timid, scared, or uncertain, her smile forced, not the one he had come to love.

She'd told him performing on a bike was what she knew.

Belle and Lucky must have taught her. It only made sense she'd try to please them. Her family, she said. One she'd adopted.

Her affection for the couple was evident in other photos, no different than how she carried their picture next to her heart. In these shots, she always had her arm around Belle's waist or linked through Lucky's arm.

The articles devoted paragraphs to their bios. Many claimed Belle was on the same level as the renowned Teri Kezar and Debbie Lawler, women he'd never heard of. If the stories about Lucky proved true, his talents were just a shade below Evel Knievel's.

Information about Toni proved scant. In one article, Lucky and Belle claimed she was their niece. She had this life in her blood.

Zach would have wagered she'd been a scared kid who'd done what she needed to do in order to survive something he was afraid to imagine.

Over the years, her risk-taking and confidence increased as evidenced in YouTube videos posted by a promotion company. The first, from a California county fair, showed Toni at seventeen, a bit less curvy than now, her hair as black, her smile a shade insecure.

Wincing inwardly, he could barely watch her completing jump after jump, the crowd's arms pumping in the background, men whistling through their fingers, women bouncing up and down, Toni taking a bow, looking beyond relieved she hadn't crashed.

Behind the bleachers, a banner displayed the town name.

Whether it was where she'd been born or had lived before her father died was anyone's guess. Along with whether the foster care system had placed her with the Starrs. It didn't seem likely the authorities would be crazy enough to do such a thing to a kid.

The door leading into the bays opened.

He hit the key to show his desktop screen, hiding his research.

Toni propped one shoulder against the jamb and licked her lips, her tongue taking a slow and sensuous journey.

His heart sprinted. *Damn, you're something.* Even in the baggy overalls, she looked succulent, as womanly as if she'd worn the flimsiest lingerie or nothing more than skin.

She pointed. "You look guilty." Her voice was low enough to keep Robbie and Angel from overhearing. "Been watching porn again?" She inclined her head to the blinds he'd closed over the door and windows.

He'd done so to keep anyone from seeing him research her and his reaction at what he'd found so far. He kept his voice equally low. "I'm shopping at the website where I got the oil."

Her cheeks pinked up. "Let me see what you've found."

"No." He closed the tabs bearing information on her. "I want it to be a surprise." Crooking his finger, he gestured her closer.

She shut the door and leaned against it, thumbs in her front pockets, stance defiant, expecting him to come to her.

His hasty departure had his chair wheels spinning. His bum leg was an afterthought, the pain not stopping him. At the door, he pressed his full length to hers, making certain not to allow any escape.

She lifted her face to his, her gaze softened, glassy with

desire, accepting everything he was and could never be again.

He slipped his hand beneath her glossy hair. A delicate scent lingered from her shampoo. He buried his face in the fragrant strands. "How's work going?"

"Not as good as in here." Her voice was beyond breathy. She cupped his ass, pulled him closer, and ground her mound against his rapid erection.

The already lengthy day just got longer.

To get through those endless hours, they'd have to take care of their needs from time to time, starting now. He kissed her hard and deep but not as much as he desired. At any moment, Robbie, Angel, or a customer could stroll inside, killing the magic.

He rested his forehead against hers and stroked her cheek. "Why are you here?"

She cupped his balls and squeezed them gently. "Don't you know?"

His shoulders shook with restrained laughter. "Other than that."

"Oh." She caressed his sac one last time and dropped her hand. "I'm going on my break."

"Your what?"

She settled her mouth on his ear. "At your house, I'm your sexual slave with no time off. Here, I follow the rules the state enforces. I get a thirty-minute break twice a day, plus two hours for lunch."

His chest bumped into hers with his quiet laughter. "Like hell. A half hour for lunch and fifteen minutes tops for your break."

"Twenty-five."

"Fifteen."

"I may need twenty."

That killed his laughter faster than the back-east tourist returning. He eased away from Toni. "Why? What's up?"

She glanced at his groin.

"Seriously." Tension and frustration tightened his voice. He didn't like her fucking secrets. He wanted to know about her. He had to.

Surprise, then caution filled her eyes. "It's a pretty far walk to Em's place. It might be crowded when I get there."

He was behaving like a jerk when he had no right. Their relationship centered on having a good time, nothing more. She was free to come and go as she pleased, to hook up with anyone she liked.

His shoulders burned and his arms ached. He took a twenty from his wallet and offered it to her. "Get whatever you want. Bring me back a blueberry Danish."

She folded the bill and shoved it in her pocket. "Do you have any change?"

"Change? Why?"

"For a tip. Thirty percent, at least. I like Em. She's nice."

Not that nice. "Tell her to take it out of the twenty, no more than twenty percent."

"She probably won't do it. Loose change she'll accept. I can leave it on the counter and run out of there before she stops me."

Uncertain whether to laugh or ask if she was serious, he did neither and gave her all the change he had.

She counted the coins, looked up, and smiled. Unlike those in her early photos on the circuit and with the Starrs, this one was unguarded and happy. "Thanks."

For a few lousy quarters and dimes? Hell, he wanted to give her more, everything he could. He fought for something to say that wouldn't spook her or him. "Do you want me to come with you?"

Something flickered across her face, disappearing so rapidly he wasn't certain he'd seen or had imagined it.

"You better stay here." She flicked his balls.

He bit back a horny groan. "Why?"

Her smile faded. "If people see us together too much, they might start talking."

He didn't care. It hurt that she did. Already goodbye was in her behavior.

She kissed his cheek, delivering her scent. "Be back in thirty." She left through the front door. The blinds clacked against the window.

Missing her already, he returned to his desk and resumed his search into her past.

As fast as she could, Toni hiked up the street and reached Em and Hector's diner. The glass door and windows showed wall-to-wall customers. Breaking the twenty there would take time she didn't have. Hopefully, the change Zach had given her would be enough.

For some reason, numerous cars rolled down the street on both sides, almost a traffic jam for Indulgence.

On the first break in the flow, she sprinted across the road prior to the pedestrian crosswalk. A passing vehicle honked long and loud. Ignoring the sound, she sucked in air so hot and unbearably dry her lips and nose stung. With few trees around and little shade, she braved the sun beating down on her shoulders and increased her pace.

Out of breath and perspiring badly, she reached the end of the historic area and the gas station Angel had told her about. Inside the attached convenience store, she rocked on her heels, waiting impatiently behind a young woman with two preschool children who took forever to choose which ice cream treats they wanted. As the trio departed, Toni broke the twenty, just in case. Clutching the extra change, she trotted to the pay phone, the only one for blocks, according to Angel.

"Please work." She fed the thing coins, sweating and

praying as each rattled inside the rectangular box.

On the dial tone, she slumped against the phone stand, relieved and weary.

During the second ring, the call connected. "Starrs shop."

Belle. Her voice rasped from age and a lifetime enjoying Camel cigarettes.

Tears stung Toni's eyes. She felt like a little girl coming home after her first trip away, happy for the known, no longer scared things might have changed during her absence. The people she loved and needed hadn't left her. "Hey, it's me." Her voice cracked with emotion she hadn't predicted and couldn't hide.

"Toni?" Belle switched from businesswoman to caring mom. "You okay, hon?"

"Fine." She fingered tears from her eyes, then draped her arm over the stand, her back to the sun.

Behind her, cars rumbled down the street. A horn honked. People strode past, talking on their cell phones. Children whimpered and complained, trying to get their parents' attention.

Toni cupped the mouthpiece so Belle could hear her. "Sorry I haven't called in a couple of days. You and Lucky doing all right? Is he taking his medication like he should?"

"If he wants me to keep talking to him, he does." She chuckled, interrupting it to cough. "Don't you worry, he's being a good boy and I'm just fine. We're both gonna be kicking for a long time to come."

Toni squeezed the receiver, refusing to imagine the day she'd lose either of them and would be alone again. "How's business? Any sales? Repairs?"

"It's been slow, but steady. We're new. Takes time to catch on. Now don't you worry."

She couldn't help it. They'd been there when she'd needed someone to care about her and now she wanted to do the same for them. "I'll be able to wire you guys some decent money in another week."

"No." Belle's sweet voice turned firm. "We already told you, you don't have to send us anything."

"I want to."

"Aw, hon." Belle blew out a sigh. "We don't want your money. Never have. You keep forcing us to put it into a savings account for you. Why won't you let me give you the number or wire you the cash?"

"No." She stamped her foot, pissed they wouldn't let her do this for them. "If you try as you did the last time, I'll just send it back. It's yours. You need it now more than I do. I'm fine. I have a great bed to sleep in every night and more food than I'll ever need. You have a shop to get off the ground. Your retirement to think of."

"That may be, but we're not doing it on your back. How many times do I have to tell you that? We want you to be happy. Lucky and me love you, always have, always will."

A tear rolled down Toni's cheek. Another fell from her chin. She lowered her head. "I love you guys too, that's why I want to do this."

"For the last time, no. Take care of yourself. Don't worry about us."

Toni cleared the huskiness from her voice. "I have to—I'm going to." She spoke quickly before Belle interrupted. "You won't have to work so hard if I help out. You should be enjoying life now, not worrying about bills. And I got this really great gig for a month. The pay is great."

Belle didn't comment.

On the other end of the call, a buzz sounded, indicating the shop door had opened. A woman asked where the convenience store had gone, her voice subdued from distance.

"Moved two blocks over." Belle spoke kindly. "Down Troop Street to the left. Here, let me draw you a map."

Papers rustled. She and the woman conversed and shared a laugh.

Footfalls sounded. Belle breathed into the phone. "Sorry about that. Where are you performing?"

Toni fed more coins into the phone and hedged. "It's a small outfit, fairly new, but the people are really nice. There's Angel and Robbie, guys my age. And there's Em and Hector. They're in their thirties and couldn't be sweeter, especially Em. She always wants to feed me." Unable to stop herself, Toni embellished, lied, and evaded.

"Wow." Belle laughed. "Sounds great."

"It is. It's more than I expected before the circuit starts. It's—I've met a guy."

Something squeaked. She guessed Belle's chair. She'd either dropped into it or had shot to her feet.

"You've met a man?" Motherly interest rang in her voice.

Another tear rolled down Toni's cheek. "Zach."

"He's performing with you?"

Eyes squeezed tight, she picked at the phone's metal veneer. "I really like him."

"I can hear that." Belle's rasp softened, her tone growing protective. "How does he feel about you?"

Sorrow and reality threatened, choking off Toni's words, but not her thoughts.

Nearly a week had passed. Three more to go and she'd be on her way. Without pause, burying regret. She'd promised herself nothing more than the means to make some needed cash and to have a good time in the bargain.

What she now wanted was so much more. And so impossible.

On the other end of the call, Evan Clancy—a sheriff's deputy and one of Zach's friends—took his sweet time answering the question.

Impatient, Zach transferred the receiver from his right ear to his left. "Come on, Evan. It's not classified information. It's public record, right?"

"Most of the public wouldn't want to know her home address. So why do you?"

Zach had no choice except to lie. "I'm trying to verify what she put on her employment app. She gave me a general delivery address in Texas. What do you have?"

Tapping noises filled the silence. Zach guessed Evan was keying into his computer.

The sounds stopped. "Same one. Must be her address. I understand in her line of work she moves around a lot."

"Do you have anything else on her?"

"Why? Is she going to be handling money there? I wouldn't advise it."

Zach frowned. Hell, he seethed. "Why the fuck not? Why in the shit would you say something like that?"

"Whoa, don't get pissed at me. I'm not the one who got arrested."

"For performing without a permit and not having insurance, not grand theft. Toni's no thief."

"Toni?" Evan sounded curious.

"Help me out here." Zach had never been so desperate, even willing to beg.

Evan made an indistinct noise. "I know this is none of my business and you can tell me to back off if you want, but do you have something going on with this girl?" He spoke in a near-whisper. "Do you know what you're getting into?"

Ignoring Evan's concern, Zach forged ahead. "Are you going to give me the information or not? Don't jerk me around."

Evan muttered something beneath his breath. "We ran her prints, like we do with anyone who gets arrested. She's clean, meaning she doesn't have a record, except for what she did here, all right? Of course, that doesn't address what she hasn't been caught for, which wouldn't be in the—"

"Where's she from?"

"What? Texas. I already told you. It's where she got her driver's license, which she'll get back when she secures insurance. She also registered her bike in that state."

"No, I mean, where was she born? What's her real last name before she changed it to Starr?"

"She changed it to Starr? When? Why?"

Zach threw a clipboard across the room. It smacked the wall and fell on the sofa. "Do you know any private investigators? I want the best. Someone I can trust."

"Why? What in the hell has she done?"

"Not one fucking thing. Don't ask again."

"Fine. She's an upstanding citizen. I get it. But that can only mean one thing." He spoke in the same near-whisper he'd used earlier. "What in the fuck are you planning to do with this girl?"

Zach closed his eyes. He needed to do everything he could in the short time they had. She'd gotten that deep beneath his skin, crawling into his soul and heart. He couldn't let her leave here with nothing except her saddlebag and nowhere permanent to go. He had to be certain she was safe with a soft place to land and people who cared about her. It was the least he could do for all she'd given him.

"I'm not planning anything with her, all right? She's alone. Fuck, I never knew anyone lived like that. She's only twenty-seven yet she doesn't have a fucking soul in the world to help her. I want to find out why. Are you going to give me a name of an investigator or not?"

"Hey, Zach?"

Angel.

Zach's heart pounded. He faced the door leading into the bays, praying Angel hadn't heard his conversation. "How long have you been there?"

He lifted his thick eyebrows. "Just came through the door now."

Zach's heart didn't care. It kept slamming into his chest. "What do you need?"

"Got a customer here wants to talk to you." He spoke more softly than usual. "Nothing bad. He likes the work. Just needs to ask you about another job he maybe wants us to take on. He's having a smoke outside."

"Tell him I'll be right there."

With a nod, Angel left.

Back on the phone to Evan, Zach begged. "Give me a name. Now. Please."

Toni reached the block that ended at the garage.

Zach stood near the front door next to an older guy with a huge belly and florid skin. The man flicked ashes on the concrete, then lifted his cigarette to his thick lips and drew deeply on it. Smoke poured from his mouth as he nodded at Zach's comments.

Toni slowed. New tears threatened, coming from nowhere.

This morning she'd been eager to get through the day and welcome the night with Zach at her side. Now the passing minutes and hours sucked away her energy, telling her what she didn't want to face, not yet, not here.

Sadly, there was no denying or running from it.

With another day speeding by, she had even less time with him.

Her stomach rolled at what lay ahead, spending next month and countless others without him. A depressing scenario, unlike the lies she'd told Belle. Toni did eventually admit to Zach owning a garage in Indulgence, where she'd been working until the circuit began. Once she ran out of truth, her lies again took over. The worst was her claim that Zach felt deeply about her, even hinting at what might be in their future.

One she dismissed for Belle's benefit. Toni didn't want her or Lucky thinking she was ungrateful for them bringing her into their act. She claimed that despite her feelings for Zach, she didn't want to settle down in one place. She enjoyed being on the road, free to do as she pleased. She craved the life they'd introduced her to, one Zach could never understand.

Belle had listened without comment until Toni's lies ran out. As she'd slumped against the phone, drained, Belle spoke. "Do whatever makes you happy, hon. If it's staying there with him, give it a chance." She made a pained sound. "Not every man's like Joe."

Toni blinked rapidly, trying to clear her eyes. Being happy and taking a chance on something that didn't exist wasn't on the agenda three weeks from now. The future she'd grown accustomed to was what she had to accept.

Exhausted yet edgy, she dragged toward the garage.

Zach shifted his weight, favoring his good leg as always. It endeared him to her for reasons she didn't want to admit or address. He listened to the older guy, nodded, then smiled.

It tore Toni's heart a little more and reached her soul in places she hadn't known existed. Every part of her ached for him. He was the type of man she'd dreamed of as a young girl before Joe had damaged her life. The kind of guy she'd longed for as a grown woman: virile and commanding, but also cherishing, generous, and kind. Not to mention sexy beyond belief.

How easily she could fall in love with him if he allowed himself to do the same with her, which he would not. He simply appreciated the novelty she presented as a motorcycle performance artist and enjoyed the physical comfort she could provide during their time together.

To him, it would be the sum total of their connection.

She drew closer.

Zach glanced over.

Her step faltered and her pulse thudded. With a faint nod, she acknowledged him and hurried past.

"Hey!"

She stopped at his shout. "What?"

"Where's my Danish?"

Shit. She'd forgotten it. She extracted the cash from her pocket and gave it to him. "Hector didn't make any blueberry ones today. I wasn't sure what else you'd like, so I didn't get anything. Sorry."

Before Zach could challenge her, she rushed into the garage.

The wall clock looked larger than usual, the seconds and minutes ticking by too fast.

CHAPTER TEN

Once the chain-smoking customer left, Zach called the investigator Evan had recommended. Keeping his voice low, he told the woman what he'd found so far, including verifying that the Social Security number was under the name Toni Starr. He insisted no one at the agency contact Belle or Lucky for more information, especially to find out Toni's real last name. "I do not want you bothering them."

"I understand and I want to help. But I need to be straight with you, Mr. Brody. You're making my job harder. This couple obviously knows her real name and past. It would be a simple matter to gain their trust and in a roundabout way ask them what—"

"No." He'd never forget Toni pulling their picture from her bra, affection softening her features. "I don't want Toni to know I'm doing this and I don't want the Starrs worrying about her. That's not negotiable. Find another way or I'll get another investigator."

"No need to do that." Something smacked on her end. "However, doing this your way will take time."

"You have two-and-a-half weeks." He stared at the door leading to the bays, alert to anyone, especially Toni, intruding. "At the most, three."

"Then it'll cost you extra for the—"

"You have my credit card information and my approval for the charges. I expect a report every morning in my email account. I need to know what you're finding out and how you're doing it."

Another smack. "If that's what you want, Mr. Brody."

Sounded like 'fuck off' to him. He couldn't have cared less what she thought as long as she did what he wanted. He needed assurance Toni would be all right after she left here, not to mention him being free of his increasing interest in everything she was and did.

After ending his call with the investigator, his feelings for Toni mounted, eating away his reserve. He called the Last Chance Diner and asked Em if they had any blueberry Danish, his favorite.

"Hector's been making them all day, just like always. You should already know that."

He did, but wanted to check out what Toni told him and why she lied.

She'd needed change. The only reason he could think of was to make a call at a pay phone. Either to Belle and Lucky or some guy.

His stomach hurt worse than his leg. Braced against the pain, disturbed by it, he recalled the way she'd given herself to him these last days—effortlessly, hungrily, repeatedly. If she had called a man, he couldn't be a current lover, or at least one she cared deeply about.

He certainly wasn't a guy who worried about her. That kind of man would have helped her when she'd needed cash to stay out of jail and to spring her bike . . . unless she hadn't told him. Just as she surely hadn't told Lucky and Belle.

Zach couldn't figure out why she'd do such a thing, unless the man, lover, or boyfriend was as broke as her.

He didn't want to consider her hooking up with a bum like that and loving him, or falling for some other goon once she took off, going God knows where, doing God knows what.

"Want me to throw a couple in a sack and run them down to you?"

He frowned at Em's question. "What? Wait. No." Concern,

worry, and jealousy ate at him. "I'll swing by in a few. See you then." He grabbed his keys and called Angel into the office. "I have a few things I need to do. I'll be back in a couple of hours at most. Take care of things."

"You bet."

Zach left the garage on an errand involving Toni. One he'd thought of during his many calls about her. A matter he'd share tonight as she lay naked beside him in bed.

Toni's conversation with Belle and the feelings she'd revealed about Zach, dominated her thoughts during the day. She was far too attracted to him, which was deeply dumb since this would soon end.

Despite that reality, the hours dragged until she could be back in his arms. She forced herself to concentrate on her work, laugh at Robbie's lame jokes, and offer witty come-backs at Angel's gentle teasing.

On the drive to Zach's house, she sagged against her door, worn out. Her tangled emotions stole the casual shop-talk she'd intended to share so she could make him laugh, daz-zling him with her personality.

Meg's had probably been awesome. Sweet, sultry, and per-fect.

Toni felt ill, hating herself for begrudging her. Common sense warned she'd never be like Meg. She wasn't cute or pretty and nowhere near girly. Her nails were clipped short, no polish. Her only concessions to femininity were her mani-cured toenails and toe ring. Neither would keep a guy from noticing the nasty bruise above her knee, courtesy of a shop cabinet she'd run into. Then there was the scar near her elbow. And the tattoo on her ass.

No, she wasn't like Meg at all.

She tried to shrug off her deficiencies, telling herself she was okay as she was, but couldn't. Envy riddled her over a woman she didn't know and a future she might have had, one stolen from her because her father had died and then Joe happened.

Her memory of his heartless smile and cold eyes sickened her now as they had in nightmares past. His honeyed voice returned to haunt her.

With great effort, she forced them away and looked at Zach.

A quiet man with deep emotions and a giving heart. A good man when there were too few around. He represented everything she'd lost and wouldn't have, except for a few weeks. An ache tore through her so quickly the intense pain stole her breath.

He glanced over, his expression neutral.

She hoped hers matched it.

He looked back to the road. "You okay?"

"What was she like?" The words spilled from Toni, independent of her brain and good sense. "Meg, I mean." She spoke softly as she would when discussing something sacred.

A flush crept up Zach's neck and touched his cheeks. He fiddled with the radio, changing channels, turning the volume down, then up. The announcer's voice boomed with the sudden change. He adjusted the sound again, this time to a reasonable level. A commercial for cattle feed came on. "You want to know about my life?" At a four-way stop, he looked at her, eyes wary. "You haven't told me anything about yours."

Accusation hung in his words.

She'd deserved that and tried to keep her past from intruding or wounding. "I'm the best damn mechanic there is."

Frustration then sadness registered on his face. He pulled away from the sign, their silence broken by another radio commercial and his ragged breaths.

She felt like a shit for bringing up painful memories. "I'm sorry. I shouldn't have asked. Not my business."

He gripped the steering wheel so hard, the muscles in his forearms bunched. "It's okay. You didn't mean any harm."

"Never. I wouldn't. I hope you believe me."

"I do." He smiled weakly then sobered. "Meg was sweet, giving, and very bright."

Toni ached at the pain in his voice. His accompanying sigh nicked her heart.

He focused on the road rather than her. "I met her in Phoenix while I was at technical school. On the side, I took some business courses at the university so I could run my own shop someday. We had the same business law class."

He spoke as if he were a spectator, not a participant in his own past, his emotions buried again.

"She was studying hotel management and graduated with honors. She often talked about going for a Masters. Both her parents have MBAs. They're very well respected in the Phoenix business community."

"Sounds like my dad." Toni couldn't help but boast. "He was an accountant. A CPA, to be exact, with his own business."

Zach stared at her, eyes widened. Beneath his surprise, he looked hungry for more.

She went hot, cold, then hot again, cursing herself for what she'd foolishly revealed. Her only excuse was she wanted him to know that before she'd turned fifteen, she'd had an upbringing similar to his and Meg's. Despite her current lifestyle and financial situation, she wasn't that different from either of them. She wasn't less.

To block any questions he might have, she concentrated on him. "So after school you guys decided to move down here?"

He made a turn and nodded. "We thought it would be a good place for me to start a business and for us to eventually raise a family."

She pictured him with a little boy, the kid's eyes big with wonder, his questions frequent and fascinated at what went on in his dad's garage.

Renewed longing for that kind of life — and him — made her chest hurt, her emotions stupid and futile. But there they were, mocking her. "She was good with kids, huh?"

"Yeah." He grew thoughtful, a wistful look on his face. "She has a younger sister, Allison, who she doted on. Ten years separated them, so Meg always treated that kid more as her own baby than a sibling."

"You still miss her." It was a statement, not a question.

He flicked his turn signal and made the next right. "I blame myself for what happened."

"It wasn't your fault."

He frowned at her. "You weren't there."

"I know." She spoke as softly as she could. "But you weren't texting, Zach. The kid who caused the accident was."

He spoke through his teeth. "Angel or Robbie talks too fucking much when they should be working."

"Don't blame them. I asked. I wanted to know how you'd hurt your leg."

He stared at the road.

She should have shut up, but wanted to connect with him, at least as a friend, and ease his pain if she could. "They didn't want to tell me, but I pressed. The accident wasn't your fault."

He swore beneath his breath. "If I hadn't insisted on one last run, it wouldn't have happened."

"You were going about your business that night. You had no idea you were putting you or Meg in harm's way. That's not how you wanted your life to turn out. That's not how it should have. If I could change it for you, I would. I'm so sorry."

His anger hung on for a moment then subsided to an

emotion she couldn't read. He checked the instruments on his dash.

"You still miss her." Toni needed the truth no matter how brutal, or how she failed to measure up to his memory of a woman he could no longer have.

He drove in silence.

They reached the road leading to his house, his lost future, the continuation of her and his time together.

It wasn't what either of them ultimately desired. He needed the past. She craved a future. Nevertheless, she told herself to be grateful for what she had, determined to be all she could to him in their remaining days. To ease his loss to the best of her ability, even if he didn't welcome her presence as much as he would another chance with Meg.

Zach's gut churned. Toni's comment about him missing Meg badgered his thoughts. How in the fuck was he supposed to answer such a personal remark from a woman he'd just met? One he barely knew, yet who had become such a large part of his life he was beginning to fear what the coming weeks would be without her.

Shit, he was losing his mind.

Hell yeah, he still missed Meg, a part of him always would. But even with that, Toni's smile, laughter, and sass were crowding out the past, dragging him into the here and now.

At least until she left.

Stewing over its inevitability, he said nothing, nor did she. He concentrated on the road, while she thought about God knows what.

Her dad had been a CPA with his own business.

Her admission had surprised Zach more than if she'd sucker-punched him. After all this time, she offered that information when she'd refused to tell him anything else about her past. Like how she'd ended up with the Starrs, people who seemed to live on the fringe of society, so fucking different than her father, a normal middle-class provider.

CPAs weren't usually into drink or drugs, but maybe her dad had been and their lives had spiraled down due to his addiction to alcohol, coke, or meth with that shit killing him. But what about her mother? Even if her parents had been divorced and her father had gotten sole custody of Toni, her mother could have taken her in after his death.

Why hadn't she?

Zach mulled it over with no answer and hoped the private investigator had already found something.

The moment he pulled up to his house, Toni unfastened her seat belt, rested her hand on his thigh, and stroked the inside seam. "Time to relax."

Her smoky tone and sultry touch pushed away his bad memories and jump-started his lust. With his balls tightening and heart pounding, he practically drooled.

Tenderness and harsh need sparkled in her eyes. She leaned toward him, her mouth on his ear, voice breathy. "Let me take care of you tonight."

Liking her suggestion, he asked the only thing he could. "How?"

"You'll see." She pecked his cheek, popped her door, and left the pickup without further comment.

He was too limp to move.

She bypassed the front steps and strolled to the backyard.

What in the fuck is she doing?

He tossed her saddlebag on the porch and rounded the house, favoring his good leg.

Her black flip flops lay on the flagstone walk.

He stopped. Clenching his teeth to the expected pain, he hunkered down near them and searched for her toe ring, wondering if she'd taken it off too.

Unable to find the jewelry, he stood and squinted.

145

She'd dropped her denim cut-offs on a bush he'd planted more than two years ago . . . another lifetime. He rubbed the worn cotton against his cheek and suppressed an uncivilized groan at its scent: sweet flowers and heady musk.

Something inside him changed, making him aware of his emptiness, so needy and deep he feared it would never stop no matter how long he enjoyed Toni. His desire might only grow worse, his craving for her intolerable and unending. Wanting to flee his feelings, yet desperate to stay and feed them, he strode down the path, her shorts beneath his arm, his mind picturing her naked ass and tattoo.

Carnal hunger tore through him, making him shudder. He really liked her tattoo. God help him, he truly liked and wanted her.

She played like no woman he knew.

She'd upended the rake and had leaned it against the house. Her hot pink tank top dangled from its tines.

Carefully, he removed the stretchy material and shoved it beneath his arm, next to her shorts.

His thrumming pulse and stiffened cock urged him to hurry down the path and sink into her hot, wet pussy. His mind resisted, advising him to slow down, make this last, and record each memory for later when he'd be out here alone.

Melancholy gripped him, halting his steps. Head down, breathing as deeply as he could, he warned himself to cool it, reason this out, and simply have a good time.

Toni's power over him was spiraling out of control. Already he longed for as little as a glance from her, and as much as her delighted cries — unique, meant only for him, no other man — as he entered her without end.

He wasn't certain if the feelings ensnaring him were because their lovemaking was still so new and satisfying or if there was another explanation.

One he didn't want to explore.

He reached the patio and grinned. She'd draped her bra over the Victorian-style bird feeder. He stuffed the item into his back pocket and didn't bother searching for her panties or a thong. She never wore either. He wasn't certain if that was because she didn't own underwear or went without around him.

His foolish heart hoped it was the latter.

He turned the corner.

A lawn ornament fashioned to look like a frog lay on the picnic table. Lucky and Belle's picture peeked from its hind legs, anchored against the gentle breeze.

The wind played with Zach's hair, dancing it over his forehead.

At the pool, he forgot to breathe, his heart staggering through too many beats.

Toni floated on her back, fully nude, except for her toe ring. She gave him a welcoming smile. The kind a man needs following a shitty workday or after a tragedy crushes him into not expecting happiness or peace.

Too many emotions bubbled up, tenderness and lust leading the way. Water licked her breasts and thighs, filled her navel, and sparkled in the dark curls between her legs.

He envied the water.

She looked at him as a friend and lover would, no judgment, only acceptance. "Let me take care of you tonight."

He wanted tomorrow, too, and the next day, and the ones that followed. He wished they'd met other than the way they had so they could explore life together and see where the future led them. With her at his side, he wouldn't be lonely or afraid. When she was gone . . .

Crushing sorrow hit, gripping his throat.

"Zach?"

He wasn't sure he could trust his voice, but couldn't keep standing here and gawking like a damn fool. "How?"

"You'll see. Take off your clothes."

Last month, the suggestion would have stopped him. He wasn't a vain man, but a woman's reaction to his scars did give him pause. Considering the unrestricted sun out here, he might as well have a spotlight shining his way.

"Please." Her soft voice and gentle smile encouraged him faster than any assurances or outright seduction. He dropped her things on the flagstones, backed up to the cedar table, and sat on the plank seat to remove his boots and socks.

Finished, he tore off his tee, flinging it to land on her things. Ignoring the pain in his leg, he pushed to his feet, shoved his clothes to his ankles and stepped away from them. Fully aroused, his cock bobbed against his thigh. It should have captured his attention, but didn't. Every time she'd seen him fully nude, he'd made certain candles lit the bedroom or bath.

Doubt returned. He glanced at his leg.

Deep purple gouges crisscrossed his tanned flesh, showing where the pickup's metal had gored him. More refined scars, these a fading red, revealed the many operations he'd endured so he could walk again. His left thigh and calf weren't as muscular as his right. Each physician had warned they never would be.

Until Toni, he hadn't cared. Now, he did.

Her gaze caressed his torso, cock, balls, and bum leg, as though it was simply another part of her journey. No frown marred her smooth forehead. Revulsion didn't flash on her face at the brutal defects he and the rest of the world noticed.

She ogled his shaft.

It thickened, showing off for her.

She pressed her hand to her chest and took him in again, including his battered leg. "My God, you're so damn beautiful."

He nearly laughed with relief and wanted to cry in gratitude.

Treading water, she inclined her head to the shallow end. "Follow me."

His fierce grin hurt his cheeks. "You want to make love in the pool?"

She swam until she was able to stand in the water, walked through it, and stopped at the edge, submerged to the waist. Arms crossed over the nicely warmed concrete, she looked over at him. Moisture sparkled on her lashes. "You're still over there and I'm over here. What's wrong with this picture?"

He padded to her. "There, I'm here. Now what?"

"I massage your leg."

His grin faded. "What? Why?"

"So it doesn't hurt as much. So you can enjoy me taking care of you."

"Let's just get on with the program." He lied, "It doesn't hurt at all."

"Sure it does." She fingered sodden hair from her cheek and neck. "You've been working all day."

"So have you. I should be massaging your feet and legs. You've been on them for eight hours."

She rested her head on her arms. "That's because I'm not as lazy as you."

His laughter rang through the backyard. "You are so going to pay for that."

"Yeah?" She looked intrigued. "Gonna spank me till I obey?"

She had to stop making him laugh. "I think my arm will give out before that happens. But tell you what, I'll give it my best shot."

Pleasure glittered in her eyes. She stroked his toes. "Do as I ask, just this once."

"This once?" She'd asked for a job he hadn't expected to give, sex he'd tried to avoid, and an emotional connection he still figured he should resist.

"Please?"

Unguarded yearning echoed in her voice, increasing the intimacy between them. Powerless to resist, he sank to his ass, making certain not to wince or growl at the pain shooting down his leg, and dangled his feet in the water. "Happy? No need to massage me. I'm not in any pain."

Her eyes grew shiny. She glanced away and focused on his thigh. "I know."

Lightly, she rested her hands on his ruined flesh.

His muscles jumped. He flinched.

"It's okay." She kept her voice low and soothing. With her thumbs pressed into his thigh, she rotated them gently. "Does that feel good?"

"What?"

"Is this all right, or do you want me to stop?"

"No. Don't." He'd choked out his words. "It's great."

"How about this?" She pressed her mouth to his inner thigh, slightly above his knee.

He moaned. "I like that."

She did, too, and kneaded the uninjured part on his leg, while she licked the shockingly deep scars, bathing them with her tongue, wanting him to know there wasn't anything about his body, mind, or being she didn't love.

Reckless, she knew, but she could no longer deny her feelings for him.

She licked the short dark hairs on his upper thigh.

He crossed his calves over her legs, keeping her close, claiming her for the moment.

Smiling inwardly, she inched higher and reached the thicker hair near his groin.

On an uninhibited moan, he sagged to the concrete, his left

arm above his head, his right draped over his eyes.

Still kneading his muscles, she pressed her face to his dark curls and filled herself with his male scent.

His breath sputtered out. He groaned. "Suck me."

She licked the wiry hairs one last time and lifted her head. "I need to massage your leg."

"To hell with it. It's fine. I don't care if it falls off." He squeezed his fists. "Suck my cock, dammit. That's what hurts."

His jagged breathing proved as much. She caressed his meaty rod, testing its weight, and drank in its beauty. Ruddy with arousal, the thick column exuded male power and life. The smooth, silky cap was tantalizingly plump. Pre-cum escaped the tiny slit.

She licked it away.

His legs bumped against her. What breath he'd managed to take in escaped him noisily.

Pleased with his response and stirred beyond restraint, she eased his cock aside and concentrated on his sac, tumid with need, tight against his body, a woman's wet dream. Rich and deep need rippled through her. She eased his right ball between her lips.

He spat out a curse and squirmed.

Not the reaction she'd expected, but unless and until he told her to stop, she wouldn't.

She slipped him inside her mouth and explored his male terrain with her tongue: the faint hairs, firm gland, intense heat.

He shoved his fingers through her hair and cupped her head, though not to redirect her to his cock. Instead, he anchored her to him, leaving her no escape from tending his balls.

She couldn't think of a better way to spend the evening or her life. After releasing the right one, she gave her love to the left.

He made crude noises, more animal than human, un-crossed his legs and pulled them up, resting his heels on the concrete.

What a picture he created. Unable to resist, she stroked the seam between his cheeks.

He struggled for air.

Relentlessly, she stole it, releasing his ball and easing his cock deep into her mouth. Not all the way. That would come later.

A gasp tore from him. Contentment followed, producing a prolonged moan.

Loving the sound, she swept her tongue down his length and eased him from her mouth.

His hand fell away from her head.

Only his crown remained between her lips, a delicious mouthful. She flicked her tongue over the slit, tasting the salty fluid and his passion.

He lifted his hips, seeking renewed entrance into her mouth.

She gave him what he wanted and she had to have, open-ing her throat, pulling him in more deeply than earlier. Her nose touched his thatch. She smelled his lust—primitive, erotic—identical to her own.

With all her will, she tried to keep her pace steady and slow, to draw this out. His coarse growls defeated her. She worked his most sensitive part, flicking her tongue over the uneven skin behind his crown.

His heels slipped off the concrete, legs splashing back into the water, back arching. He cried wildly.

Paying no heed, she focused on her task and probed his anus.

A guttural sound escaped him.

Hot, thick cum spurted into her mouth, the pulsations

mimicking his strangled gasps.

Sucking gently now, she swallowed the evidence of his pleasure, proof she'd touched a part of him. For a moment in time, she was a woman he wanted.

She hoped when she left, he'd remember her for at least a little while.

Not wanting to go there, she ignored her longing and drank him dry, then eased his cock from her mouth. Still hungering for closeness, she rested her face on his groin, her hand on his injured thigh.

He panted, coughed, then touched her cheek. Her skin was still damp from the pool and hot, frustrated tears. Giving this up was going to be so fucking hard. She was tired of fighting for things others took for granted: a permanent home, family, a man who cherished her, happiness, at the very least a chance to relax.

She'd lacked that for so long until now. And soon this would be gone.

"Thank you." He inhaled deeply, his belly quivering. "That was awesome."

She smiled so hard more tears spilled out, but she made certain to keep them from her voice, along with her impossible feelings for him. "You think?"

He laughed wearily.

She snuggled closer, content to stay here forever.

His laughter wound down. Wrapped in silence, they remained as they were, minutes passing by. A soft, warm breeze brushed past. Leaves rustled. Birds cried out from somewhere in the distance.

He smoothed her hair. "Sleepy?"

She shook her head, not wanting to waste a precious moment with him. "You?"

"Nope."

"Good. You snore."

He laughed. "Bull. Despite your insult, I'm not going to make you work tomorrow."

This was news. She lifted her head. "Why not? Customers won't come by? It's a holiday the city council thought up?"

"They had nothing to do with it, I did. And it's only for you and me." His earlier fatigue had lifted. Possessiveness burned in his eyes. "There aren't many work orders. Even if more come in, Angel can run the place and call in his cousins who help out sometime. Tonight, you're mine and all the next day. Any fucking way I want. And I do mean any. So don't even think of getting away. If you try, I'll tie you to the bed again."

Her heart sang while her mind warned he was only playing a carnal game, the one they'd agreed on. More worrisome, he was putting his reputation on the line and she couldn't allow that. Indulgence was his home.

He gave her a funny look. "What's wrong?"

"Have you told Angel yet?"

"No. Why? Would you rather work?"

"Of course not, but he's going to wonder why we're both gone at the same time. So will Robbie. They might talk. Oh hell, they will talk. Everyone else will too. Indulgence is a small town. Already everyone looks at me like I have two heads. I don't want them doing that to you."

"I don't give a fuck what they think about me."

"I do."

He rubbed his mouth, looking like he wanted to argue.

"Please?"

"Fine. I'll tell him I have a matter to deal with that involves the business, maybe a new tool demonstration, and that you called me last night, which is tonight, to say you were sick."

"What's wrong with me?"

"PMS?"

She slapped his arm.

He laughed, his frustration with her gone. "Migraine?"

That sounded too lame. "How about an emergency with a friend? Maybe an ER visit. I can make something up to tell him and Robbie before I go back."

"Deal." Zach put out his hand.

She kissed his palm. "Are you going to punish me?"

"Naw." He cradled her cheek. "You didn't piss me off that much."

She bit his thumb. "I meant tonight."

"If you draw blood, no." He examined the part she'd nipped then pulled his legs from the pool and propped his feet on the edge. "Enough conversation. Keep taking care of me as you promised. You're not through. Not for a long time to come."

CHAPTER ELEVEN

To Zach's surprise, Toni didn't enjoy him again orally. She eased from between his legs, left the pool, and padded to his side. Water streamed down her taut flesh, some trapped in her dark bush or skimming her plump folds, the rest dripping around her slender feet. With an indecent smile, she offered him her hand.

Only a maniac would refuse her invitation. He curled his fingers around hers but didn't leave the concrete. "What do you have in mind?"

"Everything."

Her throaty voice caressed the promising, shameless word.

On his feet, he drew her into him, warming her skin chilled slightly from the water. He eased damp hair from her cheek, leaned down, and pressed his lips to its exquisite softness.

She sagged into him, breasts crushed against his chest, breath catching, a faint moan escaping her.

"We staying back here?" He eased a strand behind her ear. "Or are we going inside?"

She stroked the seam between his butt cheeks.

He started at the pleasure she'd created, warmth pouring between his legs.

"Neither." She squeezed his hand and stepped back. "Come on."

As her Dom, he should have held back. As a man, he would have followed her anywhere she chose.

She led him to the cedar table and retrieved Lucky and Belle's picture. With the photo safe in her hand, she strolled down the path to the front of the house, his pickup parked nearby.

He didn't think they could screw comfortably in the seats. However, they might be able to fuck like crazy on the flatbed.

She directed him away from it to the porch and stopped at her saddlebag. After slipping the laminated photo inside, she looked up at him.

Desire danced in her eyes, along with need so pure and deep, it touched his soul.

She pressed her saddlebag to her chest and touched his cheek. "Wait here. I'll be right back."

He didn't want her to leave him, not even for a second. He stopped her from reaching for the doorknob.

She gave him a questioning look.

He made no effort to hide his paralyzing hunger for everything she was. "Hurry."

Her smile was all pleasure, the happiest he'd seen. "I will." She poked his chest. "Don't you wander off and make me come looking for you."

He wondered if she would. If some day in the future, she'd ride by on her way to the circuit and might consider stopping at this house or his garage to say 'hi'. Or if she'd be with another man at the time, a guy who lived for one glance from her, a single touch.

Afraid to betray his turmoil, he shook his head, wordlessly telling her he wouldn't budge. He'd wait as long as required just to see her again. To have her in his arms.

She slipped inside and closed the door behind herself.

Seated on the top step, he rested his shoulder against the banister, picturing her roaming the house, going to her bedroom or maybe his. Regarding Meg's photo on his nightstand, the only one he'd kept here, not wanting potential buyers — also known as strangers — gawking at his life. What he'd lost.

Don't go in there, please. He didn't want Toni to think he'd compare her in any way to his late wife. He couldn't. Toni was like no woman he'd ever met. A part of him wondered if he would have chosen her in Phoenix if she'd been in his business class.

Unsettled by the thought, he waited for her return, counting the minutes. Tension built, straining his throat and chest, stirring interest in his cock. Around him, the night bristled with life and expectation. Crickets chirped, getting an early start on their concert. Birds flew past, their wings whapping the heated air. Insects buzzed. The front door clicked.

All too eager, he looked over, surprised at the canvas grocery bag Toni carried. Given how it bulged, she'd stuffed a lot of something into it. Their dinner? Maybe the potato salad, cole slaw, and ham from last night or the makings for peanut butter and jelly sandwiches that she liked.

Zach didn't ask. He couldn't. She'd tied the red silk scarf he'd bought in a bow around her left thigh like a makeshift garter.

Grinning, he gestured to the bag. "What in the hell do you have in there?"

"Stuff."

Typical Toni, evasive as hell. "Okay."

She winked and pulled several fat, tall candles from the bag, seating them on saucers near the closest window. Using a long match from the fireplace, she lit each.

Protected from the soothing breeze, the flames bobbed merrily, softening the shadows, the same as the globes on the gas lamp, inviting the night to cloak the areas surrounding them.

She pushed the bag aside, stood, and untied the scarf. "Give me your hands."

The scarlet silk swayed back and forth, captivating him. "What?"

"You heard me." She wiggled the scarf.

He considered whatever else she'd put in the bag then stroked the dark curls between her legs. "What do you have in mind?"

"Taking real good care of you." She tapped her foot. "Unless you're too chicken to let me."

Fear wasn't what he felt. Curiosity and anticipation whispered in his blood, roughening his breaths. "You do know I could turn you over my knee in a second and make you regret what you just said."

"You will. Later." She sank to her knees at his side, her lips close to his. "Give me your hands." She gave him a seductive, coaxing look. "Let me do whatever I want."

Weakened with lust, he caught as much breath as he could and gave her what she required . . . what they both did.

She wrapped the scarf around his wrists and knotted it once. "Scoot over toward the rail."

He maneuvered himself to where she'd directed.

With her palm on his chest and lightly stroking his left pec, she urged him to lie down.

His lids sank to half-mast. He dropped back.

"Good boy."

"Good what?"

"Sorry. Man—all man." She brushed her lips over his, drew his bound wrists above his head, and secured him to the bottom rail on the banister.

To his surprise, he liked this and the way she regarded him: thoroughly, lazily, indulgently. His cock thickened.

She leaned over him. "You're such an awesome man."

Her praise and desire touched him as nothing else had. Even if he'd wanted to tease her or pretend what she'd said was no big deal, he couldn't. "Thank you."

Candlelight sparkled in her eyes. Her gaze caressed, cleansing him of sorrow, making him want her with a fervor both stunning and humbling.

She touched her lips to his.

He molded his to hers, impatient for everything she could give.

She met his request, her kiss beyond tender, the kind that fills an empty heart and comforts a damaged soul.

The moment she eased back, he couldn't stand it. "Uh-uh. No damn way. Come back here."

"In a sec." She crawled to the bag.

With her ass lifted, her pink folds peeked from her delicate curls and her tight ring seduced him shamelessly. A part she'd given to him without a moment's hesitation.

She shifted her weight. Her plush buttocks and adorable tattoo jiggled.

Sweet Jesus, she was killing him. He wanted her on him, all over him, not rummaging in the fucking bag. "What are you looking for?"

"This." She turned on her knees and held a squirt bottle of Hector's homemade chocolate syrup in one hand and his award-winning barbecue sauce in the other. She lifted the barbecue sauce. "Dinner." Bringing it back, she next displayed the syrup. "And dessert."

Zach laughed. "I like how you cook."

"You haven't a clue how I cook. But you will." She placed the chocolate syrup on the porch, then squirted barbecue sauce in a wavy line from his collarbone to his pubic hair.

The stuff was fucking cold. He gasped.

"What's the matter?" She regarded the mess she'd made on him. "Does it sting?"

"No, it's icy. From the refrigerator?"

"Oh." She dropped the bottle on the porch. As it bounced, she lowered her head to his torso. "I'll warm you up." She lapped sauce from him.

He curled and splayed his toes.

She dipped her tongue into his navel.

He chuckled.

As she followed the condiment trail to his pelt, he stretched his legs, not caring about the pain it caused. Her touch and each caress, muted everything bad, delivering nothing except satisfaction.

She stroked his cock far too delicately and worked her way back up him, licking the sauce from his flesh, pausing only to swallow and fight for air. No different than him. She finished at his collarbone and pressed her face against his neck, sucking it.

Glorious warmth barreled through him. His chest pumped hard. She pulled his concentration in two directions: her fingers on his shaft and her lips on his throat. His rod won, capturing his full attention.

She dragged her thumb over the slit in the crown and used his pre-cum to lubricate it.

He grunted in delight. "I want inside you."

She sucked and stroked him as though he hadn't spoken.

Frustrated and so damned aroused he couldn't think straight, he yanked on the silk scarf. It held fast. He cursed the fucking thing. "Now, dammit."

She kissed his clenched jaw, temple, and ear. "In a sec."

"Fuck that. I can't wait."

"You'll have to. I haven't had dessert yet. Neither have you." She scooted back, grabbed the chocolate syrup, and aimed the tip at his head. "Open your mouth."

He swore and laughed. "Just wait until I have you hog-tied."

"Looking forward to it. Now, keep still." She drenched his cock and sac in chilled chocolate.

He writhed. "Holy shit! Are you trying to kill me?"

"Not particularly. I had no idea you were so delicate."

His cock was hard enough to pierce concrete. "Untie me, then say that."

She laughed. "I'm not crazy."

He yanked his arms, needing to free himself so he could push her back and drive his cock into her juicy, hot pussy.

Unfazed and unhurried, she smeared the chocolaty concoction over those parts she'd missed.

Delight coursed from his balls to the back of his throat and top of his head. Thrashing, he jerked his legs up. His thigh bumped her arm.

She wagged her finger. "Keep still."

"Fuck that. I—"

He couldn't finish. She licked sauce from his balls.

Moans and sighs poured from her, the sounds a woman makes when nearing orgasm.

His edged closer.

Her tongue flicked up his shaft and reached the head. She licked it as she might an ice cream cone.

His legs wavered so badly, he dropped them to the porch then pulled them back up despite the pain, unable to settle on a position, incapable of anything except pure emotion.

She took his cock deep within her mouth, the heat as intense as her pussy, her tongue adding a dimension her sheath never could.

Words poured from him, rushed and incoherent.

With long, measured licks, she tended him, making him so fucking hard he hurt in places he hadn't used in years. Just as he was ready to beg her to stop and give him a moment's peace, she allowed his shaft to slip from her mouth.

He heaved air and forced his lids to open.

She straddled him, her dark curls above his hairy groin, her folds plump with arousal, slick from her cream. She pinned him with her gaze, wickedness burning in her eyes. "Ready?"

Velvet and smoke rippled in her alluring question.

"Don't you dare make me wait." His command sounded more like a plea.

Her lids sank. In the candlelight, with darkness surrounding them, her skin was a pale gold, smooth and flawless, her face flushed from desire.

She positioned his cock to pierce her opening and sank down on him.

His mouth fell open, his breath squandered, rushing out in a noisy wheeze.

She guided him inside quickly, her strong muscles hugging him close, inviting him home.

He wasn't yet there and thrust his hips, burying himself to the root, his curls touching hers. At her blessed tightness and heat, he fought for air then held his breath, preparing for her to ride him.

Head lolling on her shoulders, she touched her clit.

Oh hell, no. That was his job. He reached for her. The damn scarf not only stopped him but his hands jerked back, hitting the wood. "Fuck."

She opened one eye. "You okay?"

"What do you think?"

She regarded her groin touching his. "Yeah, you're doing fine."

"My knuckles hurt. They're probably bleeding. Untie me."

"Relax." She stroked his belly. "You can lose up to five quarts of blood before you pass out."

He barked a laugh. "By that point I'd be dead. Come on, untie me. I want to touch you."

She stroked her nub. Her pussy constricted around his cock. "Later."

Trapped by the scarf, gripped by the yearning in her voice and her sumptuous curves, he couldn't do anything but watch her masturbate.

Her lips parted on a breathy sigh. Candlelight and the gas lamp bathed her in a cozy glow, creating shadows on her smooth cheeks from her long lashes. Her lids fluttered and her pussy tightened around him.

Already, she was close to orgasm, shameless passion in her moans, her body language easy for him to read as though he'd known her forever and they'd never been strangers.

At this moment, they weren't. She was as much a part of his life as his hair and eye color and the scars on his leg. Something he couldn't change or forget.

With her, he didn't want to. He wasn't sure when she'd become a fixture in his life, their time together at work and here pleasant, fun, and necessary. At least for him.

Rubbing her clit, she pushed up, releasing his rod until only the crown remained inside her tight, slippery heat. Then she sank back down, capturing and confining him again.

He panted and gripped the rail, holding tight for her next move.

She lifted herself from him and glided back down, all while stroking her nub. Too soon he edged toward the peak. She did too, her breaths tattered, face reddened, shoulders tense. She lifted her chin.

No. He wanted to see her when she came and abandoned propriety. *Look at me.*

She didn't.

The tempest building within him was too great for Zach to fixate solely on her. Toni riding his shaft, tending to and loving him, stole his thoughts.

Her gasping cry cut through the night, followed by his uncontrolled roar. Everything else quieted around them, the darkness seeming to wait and watch.

Gulping air, she sagged against him, damp from perspiration, as he was. She rested her face on his shoulder, her breath skipping across his skin.

He lowered his arms to cradle her, or tried. The damn scarf stopped him again. "Untie me."

She muttered a sleepy, "Later."

He didn't back down. "Now."

"Make me."

He sputtered a laugh that turned into a discontented growl, his chest and belly pushing into hers.

She responded with a sloppy yawn. "You'll have to do better than that."

"How about I put you on the schedule tomorrow and make you work while I stay here and masturbate?"

Moaning, she rubbed her nose against his chest. "Prick."

He laughed anew, breathless and weary. "Come on. Untie me. I want to hold you."

On a loud groan, she hauled herself up, released his cock from her pussy, and worked on the knot, her breasts swaying provocatively above his lips. He lifted his head and licked her left nipple.

She made an approving noise and forgot the scarf to stroke his arms.

"Toni. The scarf?"

"Right." She resumed her work, succeeding at last, and slipped back down to him.

Once she'd settled, he wrapped his arms around her and rolled them over until she was beneath him. He touched his nose to hers. "Much better."

She searched his face. "Is your leg okay?"

It hurt as it always did if he put too much weight on it, especially on a hard surface. The porch certainly wasn't a bed. Not that he cared. The pain was bearable as long as he had her lush heat and impassioned responses. "It's fine." He licked stray chocolate from her mouth.

She smiled.

The candlelight enhanced her blue-green irises, making them breathtaking. Awed, he couldn't help staring. "Did you enjoy yourself?"

"Oh yeah." Happiness softened her features. "You?"

He nuzzled his cock against her. "Do you even have to ask?"

An emotion flickered in her eyes. She stroked his chest, looking at it rather than him. "Maybe."

Her hesitation stopped him cold and drove away his sleepiness. He thought back to when she'd been in the house, gathering her *stuff*. Maybe she had gone into his bedroom and seen Meg's photo. He hoped she wasn't now comparing herself to a woman he once loved.

Although he wanted to know, he wasn't yet willing to risk the aftermath from such intimacy, particularly if it wasn't good. "Are you hungry?"

She slid her gaze to his, mischief back in her eyes. "What do you think?"

Damn, she was something. Moody for a second then bouncing back, ready to have fun. Almost like a guy, but better. "Hungry for food. Dinner. The real kind with more than condiments. We can eat it out here or in bed. Your choice."

"Bed." She grinned. "I can make us some peanut butter and jelly sandwiches."

A kid's meal, not a grown man's. He tried not to react negatively. "Thanks, but you've done too much work already."

"Sleeping with you isn't work."

He wasn't sure whether to laugh or hug her and never let go. "I know. Same here, with you. What you did out here, what we did, was awesome. Now it's time for me to take care of you."

He straightened and retreated from between her legs, noting the loss immediately. Without her, the world was too damn cold and harsh. "I have a couple of frozen pizzas from Paula's." He sat back on his heels, ignoring the pain in his knee and thigh. "How about we have that?"

"You're the boss." She rolled to the side, pushed to her feet effortlessly, and offered him her hand.

Her gesture moved and irritated him. Not willing to concede any discomfort, wanting to prove he didn't need help, he kissed her palm and stood on his own. His leg screamed in protest.

She pretended not to notice his agony and looked at the candles. "Better put out the fire."

"I'll get it. Toss the other stuff in the bag."

Standing on one leg, she lifted the other behind herself and scratched her calf. "You always this bossy?"

He tongued her right nipple. She murmured her approval. He straightened. "You haven't seen bossy, sweetheart . . . but you will."

Her lids sank to slits, a temptress's look on her face. "Oh yeah?"

"Count on it." He gave her a playful swat.

She cooed. "Guess I better get moving."

"Before you fall." Even though he'd smacked her ass, she still balanced on one leg better than he had before the accident. "How do you do that?"

She regarded his cock, shiny with his ejaculate and the remnants of her desire. "What?"

"Stand on one leg so well."

Wearing a distracted smile, she shrugged. "Took a lot of dancing as a kid. I was in all the recitals. Wanted to be a ballerina when I grew up."

Instead, she'd ended up with the Starrs.

Given her placid mood, she didn't realize what she'd just divulged . . . what he'd tell the investigator to possibly aid in her search. He wanted to ask Toni what had brought her to this moment, leaving her broke, alone, depending upon strangers to be her family, but didn't. He figured she wouldn't answer. Whatever bad thing had happened to her as a teen, changing her life forever, she didn't want to share it.

The reality should have convinced him to stop his search.

It didn't. He had to know about her, if for no other reason than to assure himself she'd be safe after she left.

Which reminded him of what he'd forgotten: the errand he'd gone on this afternoon involving her. "I have something for you."

She grinned at his cock. "Yeah, I know."

"Careful, darlin', or someone might accuse you of having your mind in the gutter."

"Fuck 'em."

She was his kind of woman. "I have something for you other than my awesome equipment."

"Now you're bragging. But I forgive you." She kissed his chin. "What?"

"Huh?"

"What do you have for me? Wait, I know." She bounced on her heels. "You found something at that erotic shop for us to use tonight, didn't you?"

Not even close. Rather than explain, he crossed the porch.

"Hey." She followed. "If I guessed wrong, don't get pissed."

"I'm not. I left it in my pickup. Stay there."

He hurried as fast as his leg allowed and took his surprise from beneath his seat. On his approach, Toni stared at the manila envelope he held. "Here." He handed it to her.

Rather than opening the thing, she shook it and smiled. "Don't tell me. You took an online course in BDSM at that shop and this is your dominatrix's certificate."

He laughed. "I believe you would be the dominatrix."

Her eyes widened. "You got me a certificate?"

"Just open the damn thing."

She did, frowning as she peered inside. Her mood didn't improve after she pulled out the papers and saw what they were. She looked at him as if he'd slapped her.

He hadn't expected her response and figured he better

explain. "It's not the best insurance, but it's enough to satisfy the court. As soon as you sign the documents, you'll get your license back. We can go to the sheriff's station tomorrow and pick it up."

She looked at the paperwork.

He waited for her to say something positive, like thanking him.

She held the papers so tightly, they made crunching noises.

He hoped she didn't think this was charity on his part and that he thought less of her. If she did, he had to dispel that notion fast. "I took the liberty of paying for it with what you've already earned at the shop."

She looked at him with veiled eyes, her desire for him gone.

Clueless as to what brought on her odd mood, he stated the obvious. "You have to have insurance to get your license back. Right now, you can't even test drive the vehicles you repair. Angel or Robbie have to do that. After tomorrow, they won't."

Something unreadable passed across her face, draining the tension he'd seen, leaving her looking tired.

"Thanks." She spoke without emotion and glanced away. "I'll put this in the spare bedroom I'm using."

She left his side and entered the house, the door clicking gently behind her.

CHAPTER TWELVE

Toni stopped at the stairway and gripped the railing. Fighting tears, she told herself to quit behaving like a fool. She was stupid to have hoped she'd stay here longer than a month or that Zach would indicate he wanted anything other than their initial agreement.

She was his employee, not a friend. She slept with him when he wanted, period. She wasn't a real lover or someone he cared for.

Slumped against the post, she squeezed the manila envelope, hating what it represented, wanting to tear it to shreds.

On the porch, plates clattered, telling her he was removing the dripping candles from them, removing evidence of one of the best nights she'd ever had. Not lonely and desperate as she was used to, but soft and intimate, filled with laughter and promise rather than despair.

The porch light came on. Its yellow haze poured through the sheer curtains, warm and inviting in a place she had begun to consider home.

Yeah, right. You don't have any. You never will.

Not even with Belle and Lucky, since she couldn't impose on them forever. They had their own problems, their ages working against them, along with an economy that seemed determined to beat everyone down except the wealthy. As an adult, she needed to take care of herself without any help. She certainly couldn't expect the men on the circuit to rush to her rescue. To them, she was nothing more than someone to hang out with or a warm body for a quick fuck.

She'd live alone and would probably die that way too.

She bounded up the stairs, heart aching, tears running down her face. Leaving Zach would be one of the most wrenching things she'd ever done, almost as bad as what she'd faced at fifteen.

But she'd survive. She had no other choice.

She'd never be the kind of woman he'd treasure. Once the sport of sleeping with her wore off, he'd be far more discerning, seeing her on her way.

He already had with the insurance, a sure means of getting her out of here. His first step in saying goodbye.

Zach didn't mention the insurance again, nor did Toni. As their pizza baked, he called Angel, offering his rehearsed excuses for her and him not being at the shop tomorrow. She showered and gave him a quick, forced smile upon leaving the bath. After he'd bathed, they sat on her bed, facing each other, smelling of soap, not sex, eating their meal.

She kept the conversation light and constant, talking about obnoxious customers at the shop, Angel's little boy who was coming to visit him for a week, Robbie's new girlfriend, a real babe he'd just snagged.

Through it all, she avoided his gaze, looking at him only when she didn't think he'd notice. During those instances, he couldn't read what was going on inside her.

He considered she might be pissed he'd used her earnings to buy the insurance, keeping her from sending the funds to Lucky and Belle. Several times, he came close to asking her to be straight with him, but didn't, not eager to start a fight or push her even further away.

For the first time since they'd met, she seemed a true stranger, her mood perplexing, her thoughts impenetrable.

His disappointment and frustration mounted. So did

unquenchable need. He wanted the old Toni back, realizing how crazy his thoughts were. There was no old Toni . . . they'd known each other for such a brief time.

He felt as if they'd never been apart. Being with her seemed so fucking safe yet alarming at the same time and he couldn't figure out why.

Unwilling to examine his feelings, he took their empty plates and placed them on the nightstand. Attuned to his mood, she stretched out on the mattress, lips parted, her mouth waiting for his tongue or cock. Her manner suggesting she would do everything she could to satisfy him . . . to take care of him.

For how long? Given the way he felt now, his answer was not nearly enough. And when things ended between them, what then? Dizziness swept over him, followed by fury and despair. He feared whatever Toni gave would never be sufficient to still his sprinting pulse and satisfy his impoverished heart. The longer she was with him, the more drugged he became by her scent and touch.

He captured her wrists, pulled her arms above her head, and held them there as he unfolded his length over hers.

Confining her. Keeping her close.

She ground against him sensuously, offering the resistance he craved and required, his feelings out of control. Once he started things with her, he worried he wouldn't be able to stop.

You have to.

Someday soon, she'd be leaving him.

Though not tonight.

He reached for the silk scarf then remembered he'd left it downstairs in the grocery bag. Cursing his forgetfulness, he made do with his hand on both her wrists, not about to let her go.

With a savageness that reached his core, he plunged his cock into her snug channel — a perfect fit for him — taking her repeatedly, thrusting and pounding into her as she offered everything she had.

Except time, the truth of who she was, where she'd been, and the places she'd be going once she left here.

Sleeping fitfully through the night, Zach didn't dream, and awakened with a start. Sun streamed through the curtains. He squinted at the infernal brightness and rolled over, his back to the window, his front facing an empty mattress.

Panic gripped him. *Where is she?*

Wincing at the stiffness and pain in his leg, he padded to the hall bath. Dark. Empty.

He raced then limped down the hall to his room, cursing his injury, wishing he could walk faster.

She wasn't in the master suite either, nor in the other guest bedroom. As quickly as his leg permitted, he hurried down the stairs and checked the living and dining rooms. Nothing. Nor was she in the kitchen.

Blood pounded in his ears. His heart drummed so hard he could barely breathe.

Overwhelming helplessness gripped him. An emotion he hadn't experienced for years, not since the morning he'd awakened in the hospital, Em and Hector at his bedside. He listened in stunned silence as they told him about the accident, one he couldn't recall. He battled his mounting horror as they explained Meg hadn't made it.

Nausea rolled over him now as it had then. Toni couldn't have gone so soon. Her time here wasn't up. They had a fucking deal and he hadn't come close to steeling himself to her departure or accepting its inevitability. That wouldn't come until he knew she'd be safe, her future secure.

Dammit, he didn't want to be blindsided again!

He gripped the sink and lowered his head, recalling her face last night as she'd read the insurance forms. She couldn't have fled because she didn't want to fill out the scant personal information the company asked for. Maybe he'd misread her hesitation about her former lifestyle and she was so eager to return to it, she'd taken off.

Without her cycle.

The thought stopped then invigorated him. She couldn't get far without her bike, unless she'd walked to the main road and hitched a ride, determined to leave the vehicle behind along with him.

Uh-uh. No fucking way. He wouldn't accept such a thing. She'd promised him a damn month and, by God, he was going to hold her to it.

Ignoring the absurdity of his plan, he pushed away from the sink to go back upstairs, get dressed, and find her.

Something registered in his peripheral vision.

The back door hung open slightly. He hurried to it as much as he could and looked out.

His heart caught.

Stripped bare, Toni lay on the picnic table, sunlight caressing her flesh, arms above her head. Somehow, she'd wrapped the silk scarf around her wrists and placed the ends beneath a stone lawn ornament, this one a slumbering cat that trapped and displayed her.

For him.

He strode to the table, his leg wanting to hold him back. Zach wouldn't allow it. Grass and flowers scented the morning air, the temperature already balmy. He circled the table, feasting on her, his mood combining elation, fear, and melancholy with happiness winning out. "How long have you been out here?"

She followed him with her gaze. Unguarded desire sparkled in her eyes as though she couldn't contain her feelings any more than he could. "Only a few minutes."

Need suffused her words.

"You left the bed without telling me."

She smiled. "I wanted to surprise you."

She'd nearly killed him. He lifted the stone statue and tossed it. The thing thumped on the lawn, leaving a gouge in the grass. Next, he pulled the scarf from her wrists and dropped it on the concrete.

She brought down her arms and pushed to her elbows.

"No." Gently, he pushed her shoulder. "Stay where you are."

She settled back down, fingers skimming her thighs. "What are you going to do?"

Enjoy her every second she lived here and try to forget her after she left. A preposterous belief he needed to embrace. He didn't want anything ruining the moment, especially reality. He'd had too much of that shit these past years. He couldn't stomach a moment more.

"This." He brushed his lips over hers.

She released a small sigh, the kind that resurrects a man's hope in all the good the world has to offer. She cupped his face and eased him closer.

His lids slipped down. He drew his tongue over the seam of her mouth.

She opened it at once, her action summoning him to fill her. He did.

In the trees surrounding them, birds courted each other, or the day, with their songs. He moaned in delight at being with her in such a pleasant setting. She matched his indelicate sounds and grunted louder than he did. *That's my girl.* He roamed her breasts, desperate to fondle each, and kissed her with abandon, unmindful of anything except what she had to offer him.

For weeks and weeks. He refused to accept anything less.

Needing a full breath, he forced his mouth from hers. Her lips were swollen from his passion these last days, her skin rosy from the stubble on his chin and cheeks. The man he'd once been might have asked if he'd harmed her. The man he was now wanted only one answer.

That she required more of him as he did her.

He crawled onto the table.

"Zach, no." She pushed up. "Your leg."

"It's fine. I need to do this. Lie down."

She did.

He straddled her, his head facing her feet, his balls and cock dangling above her face. "Lick me." Edginess laced his command, as much from lust as pain burning his leg. "Touch me." If she didn't, he'd die. "Please."

She cradled his cock and licked its length, tenderness and desire in her touch.

His hair stood on end. He shuddered in delight and had to force himself to focus on her pleasure rather than his own. Propped on his elbows, he gripped her inner thighs and licked her rosy cleft.

She let out a guttural moan and lifted her ass, bringing her pussy closer to his mouth.

Wanting this and him.

He wasn't certain how he'd gotten so damn lucky to still have her here, but he took full advantage, licking her clit, enjoying its faint saltiness, the flavor a combination of her and him from last night's passion.

She squirmed and made pleasured sounds then cupped his balls and drew his stiffened cock into her mouth.

Aw, God. Nothing could have felt finer than her hot, wet heat and flicking tongue. A strangled sound rushed from him.

She took him deeper.

Her greedy and loving mouth embraced him, destroying his concentration. He struggled to maintain control, which did no good. She was miles ahead of him. Each time he tongued her nub, she licked the back of his crown, its sensitivity unsurpassed. As one, they aroused each other, delaying climax, indulging in an act both salacious and oddly sacred.

He shattered, his climax ramming into him with enough force to tingle his teeth.

She panted, her own release flushing her skin.

Well into the morning, they played . . . they loved . . . on the lawn, in the pool, on the front porch, stopping only when their growling bellies tamped down their lust.

Her mood grew increasingly pensive during their late breakfast. He wanted to attribute it to fatigue but knew better. Mischief and the sparkle he loved no longer registered in her eyes, the same as last night, as though she were pulling away from him earlier than he'd planned.

He fought for the right words to say to recapture their earlier joy. Instead, he recalled what she'd said as this began: eventually he'd go back to his life and she'd return to hers.

She finished her bacon and pushed away from the table. "We better shower and get dressed." She used an impassive tone, the kind reserved for a stranger. "We have to go to the sheriff's for my license."

"Come on." Robbie's voice was uncharacteristically subdued. He leaned into Toni and practically touched his mouth to her ear. She guessed so he wouldn't be overheard. "It's Angel's birthday. You gotta help me celebrate with him tonight."

To avoid an immediate answer, she finished writing her work order. She'd picked up her license a week ago. During that time, she'd gotten her first paycheck. With the money she'd wired to Lucky and Belle and what Zach had used for the cheapo insurance, that wasn't cheap at all, she didn't have much left to blow, especially on a party.

After her next and last paycheck, there was still her bike to get out, gas and food to buy for her trip away from

Indulgence, the money she'd need for an inexpensive hotel or the Y before she returned to the circuit and got back to her life.

Away from here. Far from Zach.

Hopelessness and anguish washed over her so quickly, she had to lean against an SUV to hide her dizziness. Not once since she'd been a scared, homeless kid had she allowed herself this measure of weakness or grief. It was too unnerving and daunting. In those early days, she'd had to be strong.

She wasn't certain she could do it again now. She loved Zach, powerless to deny her feelings any longer.

She'd liked him from the first when he'd bought her breakfast, treating her with respect, behaving as though she mattered. The pain he'd gone through in losing Meg endeared him to her even more. Never had she felt anything as powerful for another man. She'd allowed other guys to get close in order to quiet her gnawing loneliness. She'd slept with a few so she might feel connected to another human being, at least for a moment.

When it came to Zach, she carried him with her at all times, recalling his scent, touch, the impressive thunder in his deep voice, his impassioned and endearing caress.

"Come on." Robbie shifted in place. "I'll, uh, buy."

He couldn't have sounded more reluctant. She forced a smile. "You have your girlfriend to think about, not me."

"She can't come." He curled his upper lip. "They got her on the night shift at the hospital laundry. It'll just be you, me, and Angel."

"You're not inviting Zach?" That didn't seem right.

"I tried." Robbie shrugged. "He said he had stuff to do tonight."

With her. Yet only for a little while longer. Her last days approached quickly, time speeding by. She pressed her pen so hard against the work order, she tore the paper. *Stop it. You're acting like a fool.* Hanging on to something that couldn't be. There wasn't a choice except to move on.

"Sure, I'll go." Better to spend the time with Angel and Robbie than alone with Zach, wanting him more with each passing second. Desiring him endlessly, hopelessly.

Zach punched in the investigator's phone number.

Toni entered his office.

He hung up and met her gaze.

Averting hers, she closed the door and inched toward his desk. That was the only way he could describe her slow, hesitant approach. She focused on the paid invoices next to his computer. "The guys invited me out tonight. I'll be leaving here with them." She rapped his desk and pivoted.

That was it? No, 'Hi, Do you mind if I go with them?', 'Would you prefer I spend this evening with you?'

Hell, yeah. That wasn't even a consideration for him. "Wait a sec."

She stopped, dropped her hand from the knob, and faced him, her feelings masked, thoughts unknown.

He kept from frowning and forced himself to remain as stoic as she was. "You're going to Angel's birthday party?"

"It's not really a party, just him, Robbie, and me." She stepped toward his desk but remained away from reach. So different from this morning when she'd been all over him in the bed and shower. "Don't worry, I wasn't planning on having them take me back to your place. They don't know what went on between us, nor will they. I'll have them drop me off here. I'll spend the night on your sofa." She gestured to it. "I'll claim I have a headache and my noisy neighbors will only make it worse."

She backed away.

"Hold it." He didn't like anything she'd said, especially her 'what went on between them'. Past, not present tense. "I've already told you I don't give a damn what anyone knows or thinks, which includes Angel and Robbie. That's your thing, not mine. But I'll honor your feelings because I don't want them gossiping about you. If they did, I'd fire their asses."

Her cheeks reddened. "No need. I'll keep our secret."

She spoke as if he wouldn't. "Good."

Although she nodded, she looked uncomfortable, eager to leave.

He wasn't about to let her. "One more thing, you're not spending the night in here. No. Fucking. Way."

She stared, then clenched her jaw.

Finally, a reaction rather than her zombie act. If she wanted a fight, he'd give her one, grateful for the shouting. At least it would show they were still alive and they could have fun making up. "I'm working late. When they drop you off here, I'll take you back home."

"Your home."

Where the fuck else? "I'll be here waiting for you."

"I may be very late."

He didn't care if she stayed out past dawn, he'd still wait for her. He focused on the computer screen, not really seeing it. He was too damn pissed and hurt. They didn't have decades together, yet she was wasting their time with her pissy attitude. "No matter when you come back, I will be here. We'll be going back to my place."

"Whatever you say. You're the boss." She yanked the door open and left.

He glared at her retreating figure, refusing to consider her spending the night here or with anyone else once she was gone. The way she kept pulling away from him said she was already planning her escape. *Too damn bad.* They weren't through with each other. They still had some time and he intended to enjoy it.

No matter what it took, he was going to know about her

and, if necessary, help her before she left Indulgence.

He hoped.

Ignoring his sinking heart, he punched in the investigator's number and interrupted the receptionist's 'how-can-I-help-you' spiel. "Zach Brody. I need to talk to Ms. Anunciata now."

Within seconds, she came on the line. "I see you got my email. Do you have questions?"

"You sent me news?" He leaned up. "You found something out."

"Absolutely." Satisfaction colored her answer. "It's in the email."

"Hold on. Let me get into it." He logged into his Yahoo! Account and stared at the name in the subject line on her email. His mouth went so dry, he couldn't swallow.

At his silence, she spoke. "It is there, correct?"

He ran his tongue around his mouth. "Yeah."

In his mind, he repeated the last name in the subject line, Toni's surname, so different than Starr. He grinned. The name fit her . . . if it was hers. "You're sure about this?" He cupped his mouth so no one close to the door could hear him. "That it's her, I mean."

"Everything matches."

His joy soared then crashed down. "How would you know that? You didn't ask Lucky or Belle or any of their friends about—"

"You asked me not to and I respected your request. We researched her records at the DMV—the department of motor vehicles. She got her first license as Toni Starr when she was sixteen. We figured she must have been with Belle and Lucky for at least a little while before she began to use their last name. We checked old newspaper stories about them to see where they were performing prior to her getting the license. We were able to trace them back to a number of places, including Seattle."

He should have been surprised at the news but wasn't. Toni's exceedingly pale skin had struck him as unusual in southern Arizona or the Texas city where she'd gotten her license. In rainy Seattle a deep tan would have been an anomaly.

His curiosity increased a thousandfold. "What else did you find out?"

"Using her date of birth and first name, we were able to locate the records for her permit when she was fifteen. We cross-checked what we found there with the names of CPAs in the area at that time. You did say her dad had been a CPA. We found a match. Her father died of a heart attack when she was fourteen."

Zach gripped the receiver. "What about her mother? Where was she when Toni left home?"

"It's all in the report."

A few minutes ago, he couldn't have been more eager to know everything about Toni. Now, reluctance pulled him back, along with fear that he'd discover something he wouldn't be able to fix, a hurt so deep he wouldn't be able to comfort her. "Is her mother still alive?"

"She is." Anunciata paused, then sighed. "So is Joe Bauchmann."

CHAPTER THIRTEEN

A ngel stroked the photos near Toni's plate, his thick fingers taking care with his son's pictures. "I got more." Leaning close, he'd pitched his voice so she could hear him above the pizza parlor jukebox and rowdy teens. "I shoulda brought my album." He pushed the second photo toward her. "In this, Ernesto's watching his first football game with me."

Wonder and pride filled his voice.

Toni smiled. Angel had propped his four-month-old son against his burly torso in a living room stuffed with mismatched furniture. The child's dark hair was surprisingly thick and he wore a jumpsuit emblazoned with the insignia for Angel's favorite team. "Aw, he's adorable."

He beamed.

Robbie downed his Bud and burped. "Ain't no way I'm ever getting a girl pregnant and letting her take my kid, then have her screw me for child support when I can't even live with him."

Angel gave him a look. "Sometimes things happen. Stuff you can't predict."

Robbie snorted. "That's why they invented condoms."

"Even if you use them, they don't always work." Toni wanted Robbie to back off before his drinking and Angel's had them fighting. She lifted Ernesto's picture taken at Easter. The stuffed blue bunny next to him was three times his size. "You're killing me with these, Angel. I don't think I've ever seen anything cuter. How old is Ernesto here?"

He bit into his pizza and talked around the food, telling her the baby's age in the shot—to the day and hour. "I know it doesn't seem possible that he's so young there, but he's big. Doc says he's one of the biggest boys he's ever seen."

"Takes after his daddy." She winked. "So, you hoping he follows in your footsteps?"

He wiped his mouth off and grabbed his beer. "You mean being big like me? Sure."

She warned herself not to laugh at his naiveté. He was such a sweet, unassuming guy, she'd cut out her tongue before hurting his feelings or making him feel foolish. "What I meant is—do you want him to become a mechanic like you?"

"Oh hell no." He leaned back in his chair and rested his beer bottle on his meaty thigh. "My kid's going to college, the very best, not one of the crappy community ones around here. He's gonna be a lawyer or a doctor. Something real good. I'm already saving for it. Each payday, the bank takes out money from my check and puts it into Ernesto's college fund. By the time he's eighteen he'll be able to go to any school he wants." Angel grinned. "Zach helped me set it up."

Robbie rolled his eyes and helped himself to the last slice. "Zach keeps trying to talk me into getting a savings account. No fucking way. I'm still young. When I'm too old to do stuff I like, I'll think about it."

Angel frowned. "It'll be too damn late then." He spoke to her. "Once you've been at the garage for a while and get certified like Robbie and me, you'll be making more dough and you can talk to Zach about having your money work for you—that's what he always says. I'm telling you, he knows that shit like nobody else. He'll set you on the right course so you won't have to work into your eighties, like Robbie's gonna be doing."

He sneered at Angel's comment, swallowed his pizza, and burped. "Least I'll have good memories."

"That's all you'll have." Angel exchanged a look with her

that said Robbie was a fool. "I'm telling you, ask Zach for help after you get bumped up in pay. You're real good at repairs. Shouldn't take more than three months, at most, for you to get ready to be certified. I'll help you prepare if you want."

She forced a smile for Angel's benefit. In three months, she'd not only be back on the circuit but would have already been through Texas, Nebraska, Missouri, Ohio, working her way toward the East coast. There, she'd perform at more county fairs, sports events, and celebrations, surrounded by strangers, spending her nights alone, trying to forget Zach.

Her stomach burned. She wanted him terribly now even though they'd been apart for only a few hours. If she hurt like this while in Indulgence *and* his house, she hadn't a prayer of surviving the next weeks, months, and years without him.

Robbie stretched. "I'll help too."

She gave him a grateful smile but couldn't banish Zach from her thoughts. She pictured him when their eyes first met: the instant connection between them that he hadn't wanted and only succumbed to because she'd goaded him into it, asking if he didn't know how to satisfy a woman.

He'd done that and so much more for her. He'd returned her dignity and a bit of hope during their time together.

Not that it could last.

She fought tears, again telling herself she had to prepare for an inevitable departure and accept it as she had so many other events in her life.

Zach kept rereading the report on Toni and regarding the accompanying photos . . . some from old newspapers, covering her and the Starrs' motorcycle performances. Others from school events she'd participated in over the years.

In one photo, she wore a blue-and-white cheerleading outfit for the middle school she'd attended. He guessed her to be thirteen. She hadn't yet developed her lush curves or adopted her shaggy hairstyle. She wore her black hair in a ponytail and grinned for the camera, her youthful features sparkling with invincibility and joy. The kind only kids have before something awful happens to shake their confidence in a sane and fair world.

Sorrow gripped him and wouldn't let go. His rage was worse. He wanted to scream at what she'd been through then hurt those who harmed her.

Trembling with anger, he compared the cheerleading photo to the first one taken with her and the Starrs. Toni's eyes weren't the same in the second shot. Sadness and uncertainty filled them. Her smile was forced and a little scared.

No child should have to experience what she had.

Thank God, Belle and Lucky had taken her in and loved her. Zach would always be grateful for their kindness, understanding finally what good people they were. Even so, they couldn't replace her parents. No one could.

For the umpteenth time, he read information on Toni's mother. She'd never contacted the authorities to report her child as a runaway or a possible victim of abduction.

Anunciata's comment spoke volumes: *We have concluded the mother made no effort to locate her daughter.*

Disbelief and outrage gripped Zach in equal measure. He squeezed his fists so hard, they hurt. How in the fuck could any mother turn her back on her own flesh and blood? A fifteen-year-old kid who deserved a home, a parent—to have someone take care of her, to be loved.

He couldn't imagine what excuse the woman could have possibly used to allow herself to sleep at night. Unlike Toni's daily struggles these past twelve years, her mother led an incredibly affluent life. One Toni had grown up in, attending the best private schools, coming home each day to a beautiful house in a pricey area of Seattle.

An upper-middle-class existence that should have continued uninterrupted after her father's untimely death.

Close to four million dollars had come into her mother's hands from a combination of life insurance, the proceeds from selling his CPA firm, and equity in the house. It wasn't as though she couldn't afford to support Toni.

Her daughter simply hadn't mattered to her anymore when she began her new life, remarrying eighteen months after her husband had passed to a man named Joe Bauchmann.

Zach swore and scrolled down the screen, reading the information Anunciata had on him. After serving for years as a police officer in a Seattle bedroom community, he'd next campaigned for and won a seat in county government. According to an unflattering commentary in a local newspaper, he'd stolen the election because he'd used his wife's money to far outspend the other candidate.

Toni had been seventeen at the time. With no close relatives on either her mother or father's side, she'd adopted the Starrs, becoming to Belle and Lucky what she thought they expected her to be. Zach didn't doubt she'd worried about disappointing them. What kid wouldn't? They weren't blood relations. They could have thrown her back on the street at any time.

And so she adapted to their world, dismissing what she'd known. The life that should have belonged to her.

He fought emotion so deep it tightened his chest, refusing him all except the scantest breath. Scrolling farther, he stopped on the last news article about Joe Bauchmann. It told Zach far more than he'd expected to find out and provided the last piece of the puzzle as to what had brought Toni to this point.

A nomadic existence with no real future.

He couldn't conceive of her on such a lonely and heartbreaking journey. With what he'd found out, the circuit wasn't necessary any longer. She had options because of the trust fund her father set up.

One she hadn't known about.

He had to tell her, even if it meant she'd give the money to Belle and Lucky and return to them, leaving here.

He covered his eyes.

Even if he got her to remain in Indulgence that wouldn't end his worries. He wasn't sure they'd still live together, or if she'd work at his shop and allow him in her life. If she did, she'd burrow more deeply into his heart than she'd already managed to do, possibly leading them to building a life together and becoming pregnant someday.

Did he want that?

Do I love her?

The answer came effortlessly, solace washing over him.

It wasn't enough to allay his other fear. He couldn't admit he'd had her investigated. She'd never forgive him for invading her privacy.

She might wonder if his sympathy for what she'd lost was the sole reason he wanted her to stay. Her pride wouldn't allow her to accept his concern about what she'd been through. Only his love would convince her otherwise.

He dug his nails into his palm. To reveal his heart now was more than he could handle. Sure, Toni liked him and enjoyed having sex, but he didn't know if her feelings for him ran deeper than that. Bauchmann had come into her life at an incredibly vulnerable time for her. Those wounds ran deep.

Zach figured she might never be able to trust or love any man fully, including him.

A faint rattle sounded.

The front doorknob turned. He'd left it open for her, telling her as much before she'd left tonight with Angel and Robbie.

Zach brought up his desktop to hide what he'd been doing, his pulse beating too hard from what he'd read and wanting to be with her again.

Her hair skimmed her cheeks, throat, and neck. Her tank top and cut-offs no longer seemed funky to him, but shabby, the colors faded from too many washings.

Nothing like her new cheerleading uniform and the stylish clothes she'd worn in school photos.

She closed the door.

He approached faster than his leg wanted to allow and cupped her face.

Her lips parted.

He brushed his mouth over hers with respect and love.

She slumped against him, her breathy sigh smelling faintly of beer and pepperoni.

Pure Toni. Not the woman she might have been, but the one she was now. The person he wanted. He held her so hard he figured she couldn't breathe any better than he could.

She pulled him closer, palms pressed against his back, her tongue gliding into his mouth.

His tenderness receded, replaced by carnal hunger he couldn't contain, his kiss wild and needy, telling her what he couldn't. He had to have her in his life. Finally done with the past, he longed to rush into the future, but only if she was at his side.

To spend a day without her was inconceivable, a cruel punishment he didn't want to face.

His fear mingled with lust, creating desire he couldn't contain.

She accepted his boundless passion and yanked his tee from his jeans.

He wanted the fucking thing off. Her clothes too. He broke free, pressed his face to her throat, and inhaled deeply. Her scent was female and comforting, the same as her, telling him he'd found the right woman at last.

Overcome with longing, he could barely think. "I don't know if I can last through the drive home to have you."

She slipped her hands beneath his shirt and stroked his back, her nails raking his skin. "Then don't."

Sounded awesome, except for logistics. He'd never been a modest man, but he wasn't about to hold her up to ridicule. "Tourists are still on the street. They might pass by and hear."

She snuggled closer and gave him a love bite on his neck. "Then you're going to have to be very quiet."

He sniggered.

"That is if you can." She licked his earlobe.

His good sense and caution evaporated. He cupped her ass. "You have no idea what I can do, sweetheart."

"Oh yeah?" She stroked his fly. "Show me."

Fevered, he kissed her as he hadn't before, holding nothing back. Not lust, need, or a fierce desire to love and protect her that eclipsed anything he'd ever experienced.

He wanted to declare himself but couldn't, having no idea how to begin. To think this out first was the only way to go. If he made the moment special, he might be able to convince her she'd have a good future at his side. He'd never abandon her.

He drove his tongue deeper into her mouth, wordlessly claiming her, gratified at her response. She clung to him as he needed, allowing him to take what he willed.

He wanted everything and more.

They had to get naked. He broke their kiss, his huffing breaths mingling with hers and muffled conversations from tourists on the street.

She glanced from the closed blinds to him, her lips puffy from his savage kiss, skin rosy with expectation.

Excitement at taking her in here, with strangers just outside, battled with his yearning to keep her safe, to cherish her as she deserved. He ran his knuckles down her baby-soft cheek.

She licked his wrist.

Someone laughed.

He started.

She noticed nothing except him. Strength, courage, and an ability to yield reflected in her eyes. A powerful combination that would bring any man to his knees.

She took his hand. "We can use your desk. Come on." She pulled him toward it.

He held back, locked the door, and killed the lights. The streetlamp bleeding through the blinds and jamb created enough illumination for them to see. "The sofa is softer."

She smiled wantonly. "For who?"

His grin felt good, young and foolish. He leaned into her. "Not you, that's for fucking sure. You're going to get it harder than you've ever imagined."

Using his body, he directed her to the sofa.

Her legs hit the cushions. The vinyl crackled.

He latched his mouth to her neck and lapped her sweet skin, then sucked lightly.

Her knees bumped his. She gripped his tee.

"Damn." A female spoke, her oath muffled by the glass. "I forgot to get cigarettes at the diner."

"Take one of mine." A male voice.

Zach pried Toni's fingers from his shirt and stepped back.

She followed. "What are you doing?" She flapped her hands. "You're stopping again."

He hadn't even gotten started. "No, I'm not." He turned her around. With his arms on her waist, he unbuttoned her cut-offs and lowered the zipper.

She squealed.

"Shh. I don't want an audience unless it's us."

"Good idea. Get your smartphone and film this. We can watch it later."

He wouldn't live that long if he didn't get inside her now. He stroked her sweet tummy but didn't dip lower. Yet. "Did you wear panties or a thong tonight?"

She shook her head.

Since she wasn't into granny underwear, he rejoiced.

His balls and cock had already started the party without him, both pushed to the extreme and hurting like fuck. If her ass brushed against him one more time, he'd come in his jeans.

He pushed her cut-offs down. The garment smacked against the red-and-black linoleum.

A horn blared from somewhere up the street.

"Hey." A female voice. "Is that Steph?"

"Think so." Another female. "Hey, Steph!"

Shoes slapped the concrete walkway, another group approaching. Their murmurs and laughter cut deeper, rougher. Had to be guys.

Zach curled his hand over Toni's mound, stroked her slick vaginal lips, and touched her nub.

She shot to her toes and clamped his arms, steadying herself.

Now where was her ballerina ability to stand on one leg? Smug at how easily he'd unglued her, he stroked again.

The front door rattled slightly. Someone's weight resting against it.

He kept working her clit.

She growled softly and dug her nails into his arms.

Unless she drew blood and drained him dry, he wasn't stopping. "Put your hands on the sofa arm, bend over, and keep quiet."

She pressed into him. "I can't promise anything."

"Do your best." He bent her from the waist and pushed her hands to the arm. "Don't move."

"I won't." She swayed her naked ass.

"Crap, crap, crap." The same female from earlier. "We better get her or we'll have to walk to the bar."

"Hey, ladies." A guy spoke this time. "Need a ride?"

Soft laughter sounded. "Maybe."

The group struck up a conversation, no more than a few feet from where he and Toni stood. Her half naked, him struggling with his jeans button and fly. Unwilling to take the time to strip fully, he shoved his clothes down and eased closer.

She backed into his touch.

An indescribable gift.

He caressed the tattoo on her buttock, a reminder of what she'd endured. Pained at the thought, he couldn't help but marvel at her courage to survive. She'd hooked up with people who'd thankfully loved her and did all she could to help them out, to pay them back for caring when most others in her situation would have whined about their lousy luck.

She was the finest woman he'd ever known. Having her want him, even if it proved to be only for sex, humbled Zach.

He pressed his thighs against hers.

She made a soft, wanting sound, proving how much she liked them touching and craved him. He prayed it wasn't only for a few more nights.

Carefully, he entered and filled her to capacity. Heat swept through him, prickling his skin.

Breath spilled from her, followed by a quiet moan.

Desperate for closeness, intimacy nothing could destroy, he leaned down, his mouth to her shoulder. He brushed his lips over her smooth skin and left a trail of kisses that ended at her neck. With his cheek nuzzling hers, he wrapped one arm around her waist, settled his other hand on her mound and dipped over the side.

She wiggled and backed up, trying to get nearer.

An emotion filled him saying his world was right at last and fully complete. Tonight wasn't about the past any longer. He hoped it would be the first step toward their future.

Forgoing his pleasure, he tended to her clit.

She bucked into him and arched her back.

Another horn blared. Others merged with it. Youthful shouts and laughter added to the noise. Kids celebrating their existence and their claim to every tomorrow. A few voices joined in, shouting their approval at the clamor. Footfalls dashed past the front door, the sounds moving up the street and receding.

The noise became no more than static. Painstakingly, he focused on Toni's happiness, attentive to her needs. Each time he touched her, her breathing accelerated and hitched.

Lover's music he couldn't live without.

Hoping she'd feel the same about him, he loved her well.

She peaked quickly, nails clawing the vinyl, her hoarse moans pleasing him beyond reason. The powerful contractions in her sheath pulled him deeper, urging him to complete the act.

He plunged into her and gained speed, his brash thrusts meant to bring them nearer so neither of them knew where the other began or ended.

Until they came as one, breathed as one, loved as one.

CHAPTER FOURTEEN

Morning came too quickly for Toni for many reasons. One less day remained in her promised month, and considering all the things she wanted to do today with Zach, work wasn't in the equation. She slumped next to him in his pickup. "Are you sure we have to go to the shop?"

He didn't answer, nor did he pull away from the red light. He'd draped his arms over the steering wheel and rested his head on them, hair tousled, tee not tucked into his jeans, his fatigue evident.

They'd played throughout the evening and were paying for it now. "Zach?"

Nothing.

A horn blared.

He jerked, glanced into the rearview mirror, and accelerated toward the garage.

She slouched farther into her seat. "Fuck."

"Oh shit, not for a little while. Please."

Laughter consumed her until a lusty yawn interrupted it, depleting her remaining energy.

Last night had been something. After screwing like delinquents in his office, they'd ventured into the bays. The retiree who owned the Lincoln Town Car would never know what had happened in his back seat. By then, she'd been barefoot, her toes leaving no marks on the headrests and ceiling.

Next, she and Zach switched to a silver Hyundai Sonata needing brake pads. Tourists milled on the sidewalk beyond the metal doors. They were inconsequential. She'd rested her palms on the sleek bumper, spread her legs, and lifted her ass.

Zach plowed into her.

She'd struggled not to make too much noise.

He'd been insatiable. At his house, they fell into her bed well past three a.m. He'd held her for the remaining night, affording contentment she'd rarely known, and hope she might have a shot to remain in town. Maybe make her home here, perhaps with him.

Right now, she broke out in a cold sweat and couldn't catch her breath. When it had still been dark and they were snuggled against each other, a future with him seemed reasonable, even attainable. With sun glaring against the windshield and the town returning to life, her doubt returned. Once she got enough nerve to mention staying, she had to approach the subject carefully and not dump too many of her plans, hopes, and dreams on him at once.

When the time proved right, she'd ask for a permanent position at his garage. To sweeten the deal, she'd offer to get her own place, if that's what he wanted. They'd date and would surely continue having sex. He might even learn to love her.

Wanting and scared, she hugged herself.

The streetlight turned green. A vehicle passed them from the opposite direction. The elderly man behind Zach's pickup waited patiently for him to get going.

His chin rested against his chest, eyes closed.

"Zach?"

He grunted.

"The light changed."

Swearing, he drove through the intersection. "Did I give you my key to the shop?"

"Twenty minutes ago while we finished the second pot of coffee."

He ran his hand down his face and rotated his shoulders. "Do you know how to open the bay doors?"

"I flick the switch?"

"Cute." He squeezed her knee and made a left turn for the historic area. "You'll be okay while I'm gone?"

She'd die without him. What had happened between them last night convinced her she'd never be the same and may not recover if—or when—she lost him.

Cold with dread, she shrugged and tried to appear casual. "Depends." She adjusted the vent so the chilled air blew on her weary pussy. "Where did you say you were going?"

"The bank to deposit receipts, then to an auto supply warehouse for parts we'll need today. I forgot about them last night."

She touched the impressive bulge behind his fly, comforted by its solid bulk and heat. "You were busy. I forgive you."

He offered a weak laugh then fell silent.

Consumed with her own thoughts and what might prove to be her foolish plan, she kept her peace.

He pulled up in front of the shop and captured her wrist. "Don't kill yourself in there." He ran his thumb over hers. "Let Angel or Robbie do the heavy lifting."

His suggestion touched and amused her. "I'm tired, not infirm. People will talk if you start treating me like a girl."

"Woman." He took in her features, settling on her mouth then her eyes. "An unbelievably beautiful woman."

Surprise rendered her speechless. Shyness followed, causing her to blush. So many feelings ground through her, she found it impossible to ask if she could stay . . . if they might have a chance together. He was tired and not thinking clearly. After their great night together, he was grateful for the fun or simply being nice. "Thanks. You're prettier."

He laughed. "Like hell."

"Will you be all right?"

"In what way?"

"Driving. You're tired. Tell me what to do and I'll take care of your runs. I have my license back. Let me break it in. At the very least, I can walk the receipts to the bank. It's only a few blocks away."

He squeezed her wrist gently and brought back his hand. "I'm fine. I've worked on less energy than I have now and my stops are within this area. Every street has a thirty mile an hour limit. I'd risk more injury walking."

Since last night, he hadn't tried to hide his pain. She couldn't have been happier, not wanting anything secret between them. "Have you ever tried biofeedback for your leg?"

He shook his head.

"I'll research it for you. I don't mind."

He smiled. "Thanks. For that and offering to do my errands, but you have enough work waiting in the garage to keep you busy past lunch. Better get to it."

She hauled her saddlebag from the cab floor. "How long will you be gone?"

"Shouldn't be more than an hour. A couple at most."

"A couple? You said your stops are close."

He looked at her dumbly then chuckled. "I have to wait my turn for service. Chat it up with customers I see, people I know. Like you said, the town's small and I shouldn't piss anyone off. Now, quit worrying. When customers come in, let Angel handle the invoices and payments at my desk. He knows what to do." He squeezed her thigh. "I'll see you in a bit."

With no other choice, she exited.

He drove down the street. A block up, someone waved at him. Even from this distance, the individual resembled Em.

Inside his office, Toni placed the key on his desk then plodded to the bathroom to change into her overalls and rehearse her 'I'd-like-to-stay-here' speech. The words refused to come. His startling comment about her looks replayed in her mind.

Get real. He's just being nice.

The bathroom mirror showed her the brutal truth. Her hair

stuck out in every direction, each wrong. Without makeup, she looked as pale as a vampire. Faint maroon circles darkened the skin beneath her eyes. On a good day, when she was well-rested and made-up, she wasn't beautiful. Today, she looked drab and plain.

She slumped against the wall and wondered if he saw something she didn't because he did have feelings for her. Or if he'd eventually consider her ordinary, not appealing, once the newness of their sexual encounters wore off.

Her heart raced with uncertainty, her stomach twisting with too many negative thoughts.

Back in the bay, the metal doors had just finished their upward journey when Robbie and Angel shuffled inside, looking wilted. Even Robbie's usually stiff hair sagged.

They stank of stale beer. God knows what they'd done while she and Zach were enjoying each other. "Bad night?"

Robbie trudged to the john. "Drank too much after we dropped you off."

Angel folded his burly arms over the tool cabinet and lowered his head to them. "I should know better. I got a kid."

She warned herself from commenting that having a child didn't necessarily make for a good parent. At least he was trying, as her father always had. Like him, Angel was a good man. She squeezed his beefy shoulder. "You take good care of your son and see to his future, that's what counts."

"I'd die for him."

His devotion made her smile. Ernesto was lucky to have him for a dad and she wanted to count Angel as her friend. "I know you're not feeling well, but can I talk to you about something?"

He lifted his face.

Sun streamed over the hills and buildings, hitting him in the eyes.

He winced and squeezed his lids shut, his complexion

paling. "Is Robbie out of the john yet? I really gotta use it."

The door was still closed. "Want me to ask him to hurry?"

"He won't." Angel hauled in a deep breath and spoke on a pained sigh. "What did you want to talk about?"

Him helping her get certification. Having him put in a good word to Zach about her staying here.

The bathroom door swung open. Water streamed down Robbie's face and throat, dampening his overalls.

"Hey." She touched Angel's shoulder. "He's out."

Moaning, Angel hurried past her.

Zach approached the bank where he had a business account and drove by without a glance. Yesterday's receipts were locked in his desk, forgotten until he'd lied to Toni about wanting to deposit them this morning.

The auto parts store he'd mentioned was a block past the bank. He drove by it, too.

Last night, while he'd held her in bed, he'd troubled over how to ask her to stay and tell her the truth about what he knew. With her trust fund, she had a shot at a real future and could attend any college she wanted, get a business degree or study whatever field she liked. Possibly at a university states away from here.

Or she might retire Belle and Lucky's debts in the shop then take off for the circuit to support herself.

Bile rose to his throat at her doing so, driven by loyalty to the couple. Even if she didn't want to stay here with him, she deserved so much more than the uncertain existence her mother and Bauchmann had forced her into.

He drove past the town limits and entered unincorporated county. An isolated landscape populated with dry washes and hard brown earth she'd hiked through to get to his shop that first day, arriving tired, hot, and thirsty. Other than those areas bordering the washes, only a few cottonwoods and manzanitas dotted the arid stream beds, providing little shade.

He recalled dust clinging to her biker boots and leather pants, her gratitude when he'd offered his water. At the time, he'd had no idea how alone she was. He did now and concentrated on his plan to let her know about her funds and asking her to stay, while also giving her the chance to leave. If that's what she wanted.

Steeling himself against an uncertain future, he made a right onto another county road and drove to the sheriff's department.

Four cups of coffee and two Tylenol had Angel functioning enough to regain his sweet, giving nature. He gave Toni a sheepish smile. "I forgot."

She joined him at the Lexus he'd been doing routine maintenance on, checking its fluids and belts. "About what?"

"Before. When you said you wanted to talk about something."

Right. She'd forgotten too. "I've been thinking about what you mentioned last night at the pizza place. Helping me get certified."

He wiped his hands on a rag. "We'll start right away if you want. How's tonight sound?"

After work, she wanted to talk to Zach, get confirmation that he'd let her stay at the garage. She'd increase her odds for a positive response by telling him she was going for her certification and looking for an apartment so as not to crowd him. "Tomorrow night would be better."

Angel nodded.

Robbie joined them, looking less pasty than he had an hour ago. "I'll help, too. I got one of the best scores ever."

"Not better than mine." Angel spoke to her. "Passed it on my first try. A piece of cake."

Robbie snorted. "Yeah, right. You threw up before taking it."

"I had the flu."

"Whatever."

She cut in. "I'd be grateful to have both of you help me." If Zach had any doubts about keeping her on, she hoped Angel and Robbie would be able to convince him otherwise.

"Hey! Is anyone in the damn office here?"

An elderly man stood on the sidewalk, glaring at the guys and her. He wore a knit golf shirt and navy Bermuda shorts that accentuated his skinny legs. "I've been waiting forever."

"Sorry." She smiled apologetically.

He crossed his arms. "I'm still waiting."

The retired people here were the worst, wanting everything right now and at a deep discount. "We'll be with you in a sec, sir." She spoke to Angel. "Do you want to take this?"

Robbie leaned in. "Not with the booze I can smell on his breath."

Angel gave him a sour look. "No different than yours."

"Maybe I should handle him." She touched Angel's arm. "If I need help, I'll ask. Promise."

She gestured the customer into Zach's office. "What can we do for you?"

"My air-conditioning's acting the same way it did before. I expect you to fix it right this time." He pulled the ignition key from a metal ring and dropped it on the desk. "Name's Yacobi. You have me in the system."

She'd computerized Belle and Lucky's new shop. It should be an easy matter to figure out where Zach kept the accounts.

"Let's get you taken care of." She sank into Zach's chair. He'd been so horny and distracted last night, he'd forgotten to shut off his computer. The Windows logo flashed on a black screen. She moved the mouse so the desktop would come up then froze at the page prompt requiring her to log in.

"Excuse me for a sec." She gave the customer another smile and hurried into the bay area, stopping at Angel's side. "What's Zach's password to unlock his computer?"

"Meg forever. All one word."

Toni's heart sank at what Zach truly wanted, the life and woman he'd never have again. "Thanks."

Shaking off sadness, she returned to the office and rounded the desk. "Sorry for the delay, Mr. Yacobi. I'll have your account information in a minute." She logged in. The desktop came up, along with several links at the bottom of the screen.

Yacobi muttered something beneath his breath.

Not wanting to piss him off further, she clicked on the first link without looking at it. A page filled with text jumped on the screen. The word 'Seattle' was highlighted in yellow, along with a neighborhood name she knew.

Yacobi stepped closer. "Did you find my account?"

She stared at those emphasized words, unable to figure out what they were doing on this computer. Confused, she read the text.

Blood rushed to her throat and face, its heat biting her skin. Disbelief, then dread gripped her at her real surname, also highlighted, this time in blue. Feeling ill, she scrolled up and read the report title, its date, the person who'd requested it.

No. God no. After what they'd shared, she couldn't believe Zach had done this to her. What had he hoped to find? That she wasn't a thief?

With too much clarity, she recalled how he'd insisted on waiting for her last night, not wanting her to sleep on the sofa in here. Doing so would have given her access to invoices and client credit card numbers. When she'd offered to take the receipts to the bank, he'd blown her off. No one had to tell her he worried she'd disappear with them.

Yacobi let out an exasperated sigh. "What are you doing?"

She lied easily. "Searching for your account." She hit the page down key. Pictures filled the screen from her life in Seattle, memories she'd held onto years ago when there'd been little else.

Another highlighted section caught her eye. *We have concluded the mother made no effort to locate her daughter.*

Those blunt words, their brutality, hit harder than Toni would have expected, reducing her to a frightened teen again, bringing tears to her eyes. She scrolled farther and stopped on a newspaper photo of her mother, a woman she resembled closely. A parent she still longed for.

One who hadn't taken a moment to look for her.

Shaken, Toni forced down a swallow. In the picture, Joe stood next to her mother, his grin wide, soul untroubled. He'd just won a local election. The hero police officer was now a well-respected politician.

Too quickly, his remembered voice filled Toni's mind.

"Go on. Say whatever you want. Tell the fucking world. No one will believe you. You're just a stupid kid. I'm a decorated cop."

Frustration and rage stole her breath. If Zach had already called Joe, Joe would have given his cover story, claiming she'd run from home for no good reason. How she'd been trouble from the start. How he'd tried to help her, but she wouldn't listen. She wouldn't do as he'd asked.

"Hey." Yacobi's bluster had fallen away. "You all right?"

She blinked back tears, refusing to cry. Never again would Joe Bauchmann hurt her. Nor would Zach. What she'd hoped was his growing affection for her, his insatiable need to have her close, proved to be nothing more than his acceptance of what she was, what Joe had probably told him. That she didn't deserve respect.

"Hey, Miss." Yacobi edged closer. "Are you okay?"

"Yeah. I'm great." She sounded detached, her soul dead. Never again would she risk getting close to a man or allow him into her heart. She pushed away from the desk. "I can't find your account. I'll have to ask Angel to look for it."

She rounded the desk then changed direction and hurried to the board that held customer keys. After selecting ones for the Lincoln, where Zach had taken her repeatedly last night, she ran into the garage area and stopped by Angel. "I can't get into the accounts. You'll have to help Yacobi. Thanks."

She grabbed her saddlebag and slung it into the Lincoln.

Robbie looked up from his work. "Where you going?"

"I'm taking it for a test drive."

Angel frowned. "You're through with it already?"

"Yep." Another easy lie. She started the motor, eased out onto the street, and gunned the thing. The first move back to her old life.

One she should have never left.

Back from his errand, Zach entered his office.

Angel sat behind the desk. "Yacobi returned." He pushed out of the chair. "He claims there's still trouble with the air-conditioning. We're gonna take a look at it."

"Good." Sidestepping Angel, Zach dropped into his chair, thankful to give his leg a rest. Maybe Toni's biofeedback idea would work. His doctors had suggested as much, but he hadn't wanted to go through the process. He'd needed his discomfort to remind him how he'd failed Meg. His penance for having a part in taking her life. No more. What Toni and everyone else had said was right—he hadn't done anything deliberately. That clueless teen and lousy luck were responsible. Time to move on and live again. He couldn't wait. "Everything go okay while I was gone?"

"Only Yacobi came in."

He nodded and closed the man's account on the screen. In its place, Anunciata's report jumped up. Blood drained from his face.

Angel backed toward the door leading into the bay area. "Toni tried to help Yacobi, but she couldn't find his account on your computer."

Zach's skin crawled. "Toni was on my computer this morning?"

"Yeah. I gave her the password to log in." An odd look swept his face. "That was all right, wasn't it?"

Zach tried to breathe, but couldn't. He thought back but couldn't recall if he'd turned off his computer last night or had stupidly left it on with the report still opened. For her to see.

Or had Angel brought it up? "Did you have trouble finding Yacobi's account?"

Angel shook his head. "Not at all. Why?"

"I had some personal papers on the computer and —"

"Oh hey, I didn't read nothing but the account." Angel held up his hands. "After Toni left, I saw she had some kind of document on the screen, but I didn't read —"

"After she left?" Zach stood so quickly pain shrieked up his leg. He clutched his desk. "Where is she?"

Angel stepped back, looking worried. "She took the Lincoln for a test drive."

"How long ago?"

"I don't know. Maybe ten or fifteen minutes."

She wouldn't have taken that long. She worried about wasting gas and costing other people money.

Zach hurried from the building as fast as he could.

CHAPTER FIFTEEN

"You fucking idiot." Zach slammed his palm against his steering wheel. He couldn't believe he'd been so damn careless and didn't want to consider what had gone through Toni's mind when she saw her life displayed on his computer, like he, or anyone, had a right to know her deepest secrets.

Shit. Anunciata's report must have told her he didn't believe anything she'd said and that's why he'd hired an investigator.

He might not be able to make this better. Terrified of the coming moments, he drove as fast as he dared to his house, figuring she must have gone there to grab her things. She sure as hell wouldn't take the Lincoln for good. As she'd said, she wasn't a goddamn thief.

After getting her stuff, Toni's only choice was to walk back to the main road and hitch a ride to God knows where. She didn't even have her damn cycle. She could disappear into one of a thousand small towns in this country. He might never see her again.

This can't be happening. Dammit, do something! He accelerated, then slowed down, afraid he'd miss her standing on the shoulder, thumb out, her stance all sass because she had nothing else.

She wasn't around and probably hadn't made it past his long drive as yet. He relaxed, then tensed. Someone might have already given her a ride.

He took the turn to his place too fast. His Ram fishtailed. What he'd picked up for her earlier bounced in the vehicle

207

bed.

He fought for control. The Lincoln was here, parked in the shade near the house. He prayed she was still inside.

Teeth gritted against pain, he took the stairs two at a time, hurried down the hall, and stopped at the door to her bedroom.

His hope soared then collapsed.

She'd changed into her black tank top and leather pants, her overalls tossed to the side on the floor. Her profile was to him. Tears slipped down her face. She stuffed her meager things into the saddlebag.

His heart tore. He stepped closer. The floor groaned beneath his weight.

She didn't look up. "I wasn't planning to steal the Lincoln." Her voice was more gravelly than smoky. She cleared it. "The key is on the dressing table, along with cash for the gas I used to get here. I'm not a thief."

"Toni."

She grabbed the key and crumpled bills and brought them to him, avoiding his gaze. "Here. Take it."

"I didn't think you'd stolen the car. I'd never—"

"Just. Take. It."

"No."

She dropped the things on the mattress. "I'll be out of here in a sec."

If she left, he didn't know what he'd do. How he'd be able to survive without her touch, scent, heat, voice, everything that made her who she really was. His sorrow was so profound, he thought he might die. "You don't have to go. Please, listen to me. I've never had any doubt about your honesty. *Never.* I hired an investigator because I wanted to know about you, where you came from, your people, why you ended up without anyone except the Starrs. You wouldn't tell me anything about yourself."

She stuffed another tank top into the saddlebag. Tears dripped from her chin. "Maybe that's because I didn't want you to know."

"I understand that . . . at least I do now."

She sagged. "Because you talked to Joe?" Her voice sounded so small. "Because he told you about me?"

"I didn't speak to him."

Surprise flashed on her face. She looked at him then glanced away.

He edged closer, wanting to touch her, afraid to try. "Even if we had talked, I wouldn't have believed anything he said."

A tank top slipped from her hand. She trembled from her wrenching sobs.

Anguished, he crossed to her.

She backed away from his touch. "Don't." Her voice shook. "No matter what the investigator found out or what Joe would have said, you have no idea who I am."

He stepped back and used his gentlest voice. "I knew enough even before I got the report. You're a remarkable woman. One of the finest I've ever known."

She shook her head, her chest heaving with her ragged breaths.

He had to reason, desperate to make her understand. "I was worried about you not having enough money or anyone to help. Weeks ago, I'd gone online and found pictures of you with Belle and Lucky. Given the dates on the pictures, I knew you were still a kid when you hooked up with them after you ran away from home, and—"

"Dammit, I didn't run away!" Trembling, she wrapped her arms around herself. "I wanted to stay more than anything, but my mother told me I had to leave. She had a choice between Joe and me. She chose him."

The moment the words left Toni's mouth every horrible moment she'd lived rushed back, as painful as they'd been twelve years earlier. Time didn't do shit to heal wounds. It lay in wait, eager to rip them open again.

Confusion flooded Zach's face. "Bauchmann didn't . . ." His gaze turned inward. "I read—that is, I thought . . ." Horror replaced his bewilderment. "You were told to leave your home when you were only a kid?"

Memories returned from that awful day, the anger then indifference on her mother's face. "It was a long time ago." She pretended to shrug it off. "Despite what she did, I don't blame her."

"How could you not?" Pain laced his words. "I don't mean to be unkind, but how could any mother have done that to her own child?"

Fresh tears filled her eyes. "You don't understand. She'd had it tough growing up in foster care. By the time she was eighteen, she'd lived in twenty different homes. It made her afraid to share anyone's love. When my father was still alive, she wanted him all to herself. She saw me as competition, not her daughter."

Zach looked ill. "Oh my God."

"It wasn't all bad." She didn't want him to misunderstand or pity her. Homeless kids she'd met on the road had it far worse than she ever did. "My dad was a good guy. Whenever my mom was busy with her friends, he'd do stuff with me . . . fishing, camping, sports events. Stuff my mom didn't like. I didn't either, but it was my only chance to be with him."

"I'm so sorry."

Her mouth trembled. "I still miss him." The pain was always worse at night when she was alone. These last weeks had been her one reprieve. "When he passed, my mom fell apart even more than I did. She'd always needed someone to take care of her, so I promised I would."

"Oh, baby, you were only a kid."

She swiped tears from her cheeks. "I didn't mind. I would have done anything for her, just so she'd love me. She started to for a little while." Her shoulders shook on a new sob, her voice shaking with it. "We did things together. We talked. She depended upon me for almost a year. And then she met Joe."

With his name, Toni stepped back, instinctively trying to distance herself from what he'd done. Ruthlessly, the events returned, hounding her.

Zach searched her face. "What happened?"

She shook her head, having said too much already, details only Belle and Lucky knew. It was time for her to leave here. She resumed packing to leave for the next town, hopefully another job, then get her bike from impound and leave for the circuit.

Zach eased the tank top from her. "What happened?" Barely controlled rage sounded in his voice. "What did he do to you?"

A shiver tore through her. "Nothing. I wouldn't let him." She backed up. "It's over. Completely forgotten."

"It's killing you. It stole your adolescence and future."

She shook her head to refute his words even as tears streamed down her face. "I'm all right. I can take care of myself."

"Why should you have to?"

She turned away.

"Toni, please. Talk to me. Tell me how I can help."

"You can't. It's too late. He . . ." She couldn't continue and struggled for breath.

Zach neared. "What?"

She wanted to run, but couldn't move. Years filled with uncertainty, loneliness, and loss came crashing down, the cockiness she'd tried so hard to maintain fading like smoke, leaving her too young again and vulnerable. "When he came into our lives nothing was ever the same." She couldn't look at Zach, shamed by the past. "I shouldn't be telling you this."

"I want to know. Please."

It was easier to lie, evade, and pretend she was something she hadn't been for a long time: loved, respected, cherished.

Now, it was too late. The investigator had stripped away the last of Toni's pride, leaving her with nothing except the truth. "I don't want you thinking less of me."

"I won't. I couldn't. Given the woman you are, it's impossible."

"You don't know what happened. You have no idea what kind of man Joe is." She faced Zach. The hardest thing she'd ever done. His opinion mattered. If he found her lacking, she'd carry that with her always. "At first, he was super nice, taking an interest in my school activities. He asked me to watch sports with him like I did with my dad. He said one day we could go camping, and —"

She couldn't say more about his con and held up her hand to keep Zach from touching her. She didn't want to risk his comfort. It was too precious. Having his compassion for a few moments more only to lose it would make things harder.

"What happened?" His face darkened from anger. "What did he try to do?"

"Nothing at first. Then, he started coming around the house when my mom was out. In the beginning, I didn't think it was weird. He talked about my school work and helped me with math and science."

She hugged herself again. "One night when my mom was at her weekly book club, he showed up. I was telling him about a pop quiz I'd passed. He acted like it was the best news he'd ever heard, then slipped his arm around my waist and held me like no adult man ever had. I froze. I didn't want him touching me, but I didn't want to hurt his feelings either. I was afraid he'd tell my mom and she'd be angry with me.

Before I knew what was happening, he tried to kiss me."

Zach's jaw tightened.

Toni's own confusion and horror returned so viciously, she got nauseous. "I pushed him away, but he kept coming at me. Finally, I screamed for him to stop. I punched his chest. I told him I was going to tell my mom." She recalled his mean smile at her threat and his amusement. "He basically told me I could tell the world and they wouldn't believe a dumb kid over a respected cop."

She pulled in her shoulders, the same as she had so long ago whenever he was near. "He said if I breathed a word about what happened, he'd make me pay. He could easily convince any court that I was an out-of-control kid. He'd have me locked away until I was twenty-one. He warned I better do exactly what he wanted or he'd make my life a living hell."

Shivering at the memory, she tightened her arms around herself. "After his threat, he smiled like nothing had happened then left. I didn't know what to do. What he'd done and said was so surreal and different from how he'd acted before, I wondered if I'd imagined it. When my mom came home, I didn't tell her anything. I wasn't certain how to begin or how she'd react.

"Weeks passed. School was over for the year. During that time, Joe only came by when my mom was there. He never brought up that one incident and behaved as he had before it happened. I started to relax, thinking maybe I had overreacted and he hadn't said the things he did."

Her breath caught. She struggled for air.

Zach stepped closer then retreated the same distance, looking uncertain what to do.

His indecision and worry made her love him even more. A foolish and useless reaction, the same as hoping her mother would someday want her. "Two months after he'd tried to kiss me, he showed up at the house again when my mother was gone, using the key she'd given him. I was in the shower and hadn't heard him come inside. When I opened the bathroom door, wearing only a towel, he was in the hall with his shirt off."

The recollection wrenched a low moan from her, a sound of feral pain. "I slammed the door and turned the lock. He laughed — this low nasty sound. He said I was far too modest. That he'd show me what a real man could do, how he could make me come so hard I wouldn't be able to get enough of it.

"I sank to the floor and huddled against the wall, knees to my chest, my hands over my ears, but I could still hear him. He told me he'd asked my mom to marry him and she'd said yes. In a few months, he'd be living in the same house and I wouldn't be able to get away from him then.

"I couldn't stop crying. To keep him from hearing me, I pressed my face into my shoulder. Finally, he got really pissed and ordered me to come out. He said if I didn't, he'd tell my mom I came onto him. She'd believe him over me. And no one — not the cops, court, or anyone else — would take my word over his. He said I could make it easy on myself and have a good time or he'd do everything in his power to hurt me."

Zach's chest heaved with his strained breaths.

She lowered her face. "When he finally stopped talking, I wasn't certain if he'd left or if he was waiting for me in the hall. I stayed in the bath for hours, too afraid to say anything or come out. It was only when I heard the front door slam and my mom saying she was home that I ran downstairs, sobbing."

At the awful pictures playing in her mind, she squeezed her lids and tried to keep from crying but couldn't. "I told her what he'd done and begged her not to marry him. When she didn't say anything, I said he'd kissed me a few weeks back and felt me up, warning me what would happen if I told her or anyone else.

"While I was still talking, she slapped me and called me a liar. I backed away from her, but she grabbed my arm and hit me again, accusing me of having stolen my father from her and that I was doing the same thing with Joe, wanting to ruin her happiness. She said Joe had already told her he'd caught me with drugs and that I was getting out of control.

"I tried to tell her it was all lies. I'd never taken any drugs. I hadn't even had booze with my friends, but she wouldn't listen to me. She said Joe had shown her the drugs he'd found in my backpack. Because he loved her, he promised not to turn me in. We'd have a talk instead and he'd straighten me out. She said it obviously hadn't worked and that the drugs were making me lie and say these terrible things about him. She told me I deserved to be in juvey hall and if I didn't get out of her house, she'd call the authorities herself."

Toni's pulse quickened, weakening her legs. "I begged her not to throw me out. She was the only relative I had. There were no grandparents or aunts and uncles. I had no place to go. She said I should have thought of that before I caused so much trouble.

"She went to my room. I ran after her crying and begging. She threw some of my things into a duffel bag I'd used for sleepovers at my friends' houses. She told me to get dressed and get out or she'd call Joe to make certain I did."

Fierce heartache wracked her, making her hurt everywhere.

Zach's face tightened in pain. "Where did you go?"

"That first night I stayed at my best friend's house. I didn't tell her what had happened. I was too ashamed and afraid. I thought if she told her mom, Joe would find out and he'd have me arrested for drugs. The next day and the next, I called my mom repeatedly, promising her I'd be whatever way she wanted. I wouldn't cause any trouble, ever. Each time, she told me not to bother her and hung up. Finally, she stopped answering the phone and never returned my messages. During the remainder of the summer, I stayed with my friends, lying to their parents about my mom being on a vacation with Joe. That she didn't want me in the house by myself. Eventually, though, I had to leave."

Shame and grief made the hideous past come alive again. Her breathing sounded too loud. "I didn't think anyone would believe me over him, so I was afraid to go to my friends' parents. Talking to my teachers wasn't possible. It wasn't like I could go back to school. I didn't have any clothes to wear or money for tuition. I started to hang out with some older kids who were homeless like me. They said I could make some cash working at a fair in town. There'd be food to eat and a place to stay at night.

"Three days later, I met Belle and Lucky. When I asked if I could do odd jobs for them so I could buy something to eat and pay for a place to stay, they let me sleep in their trailer. They shared their meals with me and were so damned sweet." She covered her face, her love for them overwhelming her. "I need a sec."

"Take all the time you want. I'm not going anywhere."

His effortless support brought more tears, but she finally composed herself, needing to prepare for the future, her endless days away from here. "Eventually, I told Lucky and Belle what had happened with my mother and Joe. Not once did they judge. Nor did they threaten to call the police or social services. Neither of them trusted the authorities. They asked if I had a place to go after the fair left. When I told them I didn't, they said I could come with them if I wanted. They'd help me all they could. And they did."

She returned to her saddlebag to continue packing. "A year later, I returned to Seattle for the same fair. The city was just as I remembered yet so different too. On the second night we were in town, I rode my cycle to my old house. I really thought things would have changed and my mom would have missed me."

The loss she'd felt for so long deepened. "I was trying to get enough courage to ring the bell when the dining room light came on. I could see her and Joe from the side window. They were putting out plates for their dinner." She recalled her mother's radiant smile, how she touched his arm, and laughed at whatever he'd said. "She looked happier with him than she'd ever been with me. No matter what I had hoped, she didn't want me to return. So, I didn't. I never saw her or my house again."

She buckled her saddlebag, hauled it and her jacket off the mattress, and grabbed her helmet. "You have my general delivery address in Texas. Please send my last check there."

"Toni, wait."

Before he could stop her or she was foolish enough to stay and hope for his love, she ran from the bedroom and bolted for the stairs.

She was halfway down the flight by the time Zach got to the landing, his leg throbbing from his quick strides. "You don't have to go!"

She stopped but kept her back to him. "I don't want your pity. I won't accept your charity."

"I'm not offering it. I don't want you to go."

She rushed to the front door.

"Dammit, Toni, I love you!"

Too late. The door clicked behind her.

He hurried down the stairs, white hot pain streaking from his thigh to his hip and chest. Panting, he yanked open the door.

She'd stopped on the porch and stared at her cycle propped

on his pickup bed . . . the reason he'd gone to the sheriff's department. He'd planned to tell her today how he felt, but also wanted to give her a means to escape if she didn't feel as strongly about him.

Unwilling to let her flee, he rushed outside. "Please don't run away. My leg's so fucked up I don't know if I could catch you."

She looked at his thigh, her face scrunched with new tears, and dropped her saddlebag and helmet. Hands to her mouth, she quieted her agonized cry.

He risked a step toward her, his knee and thigh burning. "I don't want you to go. Please don't. I love you."

Her eyes rounded. She shook her head.

His heart fell. Sorrow urged him to go inside and escape the intense pain her further rejection would bring. A greater part of him couldn't leave her side. "I'd hoped you wanted me as much as I want—"

"You love Meg! I'm not anything like her."

"Oh baby, I don't want you to be. You're more than I ever hoped for." He joined her, but didn't dare touch. Sagged against the post, he took the weight off his bad leg and breathed hard.

Toni touched his leg then dropped her hand. "Are you okay?"

"I will be if you'll just listen to me. My feelings for you don't have anything to do with Meg. Nor is it because I'm pitying you or offering charity. Believe me, I'm not. I couldn't be more selfish about this—I love you so fucking much it's making me crazy."

He gulped air. "I'm guessing you didn't read everything in the investigator's report. Months ago, the authorities arrested Bauchmann on a series of molestation charges. He's awaiting trial as he should have been before he tried anything with you."

Zach hesitated in telling her the full truth but didn't have the right to keep it from her. "Sad to say, your mother's still supporting his innocence. But your father did love you. He left you a trust fund. With the accrued interest, it's over a hundred thousand dollars. You don't need my charity. Hell, you don't need anyone's."

She stared, not saying anything, her face unbelieving.

"All you have to do is claim it. You can use some to go to college and become whatever you want. Or you can give the money to Belle and Lucky. Whatever you decide, you don't have to return to the circuit. If you can manage it, I'd like you to stay here with me and give me a chance to be your family."

She covered her mouth and wept.

"Is that a yes?"

"Are you sure?"

"About wanting to be with you? Hell, yeah. Why else would I have run after you when I can't run?"

She looked at her cycle.

He'd forgotten about it. "Before you left the shop and came here, I'd planned to tell you how I felt. I wanted to give you a means to escape if you didn't want to stay, so I picked up your bike. All I ask is that you're happy. I'll accept whatever you decide."

She rushed to him and slipped her arms around his waist. "You make me happy! You always have!"

His throat tightened with emotion. Gently and tenderly, he held her close.

She squeezed him. "You really love me?"

Her surprise broke his heart. "I'd die without you. You gave me back my life."

She trembled "I've loved you from the moment you bought me breakfast at Em's. This morning I asked Angel to help me get certified. I was going to beg you to let me stay."

"Oh, Toni." He rubbed her back. She seemed so fragile yet

so strong, a wondrous combination. "You don't have to get certified. You don't have to work in the shop. Go to college, be whatever you want to be. Just don't leave my life."

She pressed her face against his throat, her breath warming his skin. "I want to stay at the garage, please. I want to be close to you. I'll give you part of my trust fund to help your business."

"No. I don't want anything except you. Give the money to Belle and Lucky. I know you worry about them."

"I can't help it." Tears thickened her voice. "They're getting old. Lucky's health isn't that good. Their business may not make it. I want to do whatever I can to make their lives easier. They were so kind to me."

"I know." He stroked her hair. "Someday soon, we'll visit them, or we'll have them over here for an extended stay if that's what you want. I'm taking the house off the market. I know you love it here. I want it to be your home for always."

She held him as a drowning person would, the same as he hugged her. "You don't have to do that. I'd planned to tell you I was going to get my own apartment so I wouldn't crowd you."

"Uh-huh. No fucking way. You're staying here." Before she could argue, he captured her mouth, his kiss deep and impassioned.

A faint moan rose from her. Greedily, she sucked his tongue and cupped his face, keeping him close.

They kissed themselves breathless.

At last, he eased away. "Don't move." He pulled the 'For Sale' sign off its hooks and flung it onto the grass.

Back at her side, he held her close. "We've got a lot to talk about. I'll call the shop and let Angel know we're not coming in for the rest of the day."

She lifted her face to his. Her eye color was deeper from her tears, the tint the most dazzling he'd ever seen, her love for him unguarded.

He silently thanked whatever god had sent her his way then assumed his Dom pose, wanting to tease. They'd had enough sadness this morning to last two lifetimes. "You're still out here. I said inside. Now."

Despite her puffy lids and the tears still rolling down her cheeks, mischief stirred in her gaze. "Oh yeah?" Her throaty voice was ballsy, pure Toni.

"Yeah."

She smiled. "Make me."

EPILOGUE

Eleven months later . . .

Before summer started and fried Arizona to a crisp, Toni wanted to have a lawn party to celebrate her certification, Angel's reconciliation with Ernesto's mother, Robbie's raise, and Belle and Lucky doing well enough to hire a full-time employee to watch the shop in their absence.

The events didn't happen at once, but combining them into one bash was the practical thing to do. Even with the garage turning a solid profit, she didn't want to waste her and Zach's dough.

On Valentine's Day he'd asked her to marry him. Her yes was a given. She'd suggested they drive to Vegas and do the deed that night.

He nixed the idea wanting a late August wedding.

She'd made a face. "Why? It's godawful hot then."

"I know. That means fewer tourists and locals in the area. The shop will be slow and we'll be able to take off for a couple of weeks. No camping or sports events, I promise. Ever see Paris?"

He had to be kidding. "No, you?"

"Never wanted to go before. Now I do, with you."

Daily, he proved he adored her as much as she did him. Even when they argued on occasion, they never exchanged mean words. They gave each other space and cooled down, then discussed their differences and compromised.

He delivered beers to Belle and Lucky. They lounged near

the pool, soaking up the blessedly dry weather, soft breeze, and the *Viva Las Vegas* soundtrack that played. They'd refused the money her father left. Rather than argue, she had Zach's attorney set up a trust fund for them to use if they changed their mind. Lucky tickled Ernesto's belly. The sweet little guy laughed shrilly. Belle held him on her lap and warned Angel she might not give him back. His mother and Robbie's girlfriend enjoyed the water. The guys talked motors and repairs.

Toni would have, too, but as the hostess, she insisted on helping Hector and Em at the grill. "I don't know why you guys won't let me do this. It's your day off. It's a *party*. You're guests and are supposed to relax."

Em bumped her arm. "We are. We're keeping you from ruining the food."

"I'm not that bad."

Hector wiped sweat from his brow. "Thank God, Zach hired you. If I had . . ." He shivered.

Toni laughed and lifted her hands. "Point taken. Scream if you need me to show you where stuff is."

"Don't worry, we'll find it." Em kissed her cheek. "Enjoy yourself, hon. You've earned it."

She'd been the first to cheer Toni and Zach's relationship and was like a mom to her, the same as Belle.

Toni sat between her and Zach, holding his hand.

He kissed her knuckles. "Doing okay?"

Relaxed and happy, she nodded. People she loved surrounded her, the man she adored at her side. Their home filled with laughter and love.

What her dad would have wanted for her.

He could rest easy now because she had a family she could always count on. And a future she craved.

ABOUT THE AUTHOR

I'm an Amazon and international bestselling author who writes passionate romance for every taste — heat with heart — for traditional publishers (NY) and indie. Booklist, Publisher's Weekly, Romantic Times and numerous online sites have praised my work. I've won Readers' Choice Awards, was named a finalist in the EPIC competition, received a Book of the Year award, The Golden Nib Award, awards of merit in the RWA Holt Medallion competitions, and second place in the NEC RWA contests. I'm featured in the Novel & Short Story Writer's Market. Before penning romances, I worked at a major Hollywood production company in Story Direction. My romance genres include erotic, erotica, romcom, historical, contemporary, PNR, scifi, and suspense.

Website Link (and Social Media Links):

Website/Blog: http://tinadonahuebooks.blogspot.com/
FB Fanpage:
https://www.facebook.com/DonahueTina1/
Newsletter: http://tinadonahuebooks.blogspot.com/p/newsletter.html
BookBub: http://bit.ly/2phWWDu
Instagram: https://www.instagram.com/tinadonahuebooks/
Goodreads: http://bit.ly/1wFmIu6
Twitter: https://twitter.com/tinadonahue
Facebook: http://on.fb.me/1Dl8DHy

Triberr: http://bit.ly/1CE2ec7
Pinterest: http://bit.ly/1yFLeMx
Amazon author page: http://amzn.to/1ChWFkO
TRR: http://bit.ly/1vb7eEc
Sweet 'n Sexy Divas: http://bit.ly/1ChWN3K
Romance Books 4 US: http://bit.ly/1JPtfeS

www.ingramcontent.com/pod-product-compliance
Lightning Source LLC
Chambersburg PA
CBHW070622130626
46556CB00001B/445